A RABBI, A LADY, AND A GUN

BY

JAMES A. MOHS

Green Ivy Publishing
1 Lincoln Centre
18W140 Butterfield Road
Suite 1500
Oakbrook Terrace IL 60181-4843
www.greenivybooks.com

ISBN: 978-1-945650-25-3

For

My parents, Edward "Ray" and Bernina Mohs

My children and grandchildren

And for my wife, Nancy, always my sweet bride

CHAPTER 1

If you don't look close you'll miss it. Exactly 48.8 miles southwest of Billings, Montana, on Highway 212 there is an unmarked dirt road. It is perhaps better described as two ruts separated by clumps of grass, and it leads west into the foothills of the Beartooth Mountains. The only indication there is anything at the end of this road is a small weathered and cracked board hanging loosely on a tilted pine post. On close inspection you will see the letters RDLC carved into the decaying board. A single sway-backed line hangs between poles parallel to the road. This is where Roberto DeLaCroix has lived since returning from the Viet Nam War in 1970.

Known as Rob to his family, young Roberto enlisted in the Army right out of high school. He told his family he was not going to college like his older brother and sister because he felt a calling, the need to support the United States in its efforts to thwart Communism.

During his interview with the Army recruiter, Roberto told him he wanted to be a member of the Special Forces because it was just the best way to get things done. After basic training he was enrolled in the Army's Airborne School and, upon successful completion, he received his silver wings. Driven by his innate and learned survival skills, he strived to live up to the Special Forces motto: *De Oppresso Liber.* Liberate the Oppressed. He would always remember the intense pride he felt when he marched in the graduation ceremonies wearing his green beret.

He was assigned to Company C, 5th Special Forces group (Airborne), 1st Special Forces. The nightmares began after a long April night during his second tour. Sergeant First Class DeLaCroix was acting as the senior Special Forces leader of an organized assault force given the mission of rescuing trapped Army advisers near the Luong Pho Valley. The misery of the black cloud-covered night was intensified by constant light rain. The steady drip of raindrops was accompanied by the buzzing of the omnipresent mosquitoes. And the godforsaken leeches. Rest was impossible, but needed, after two straight days of humping through the jungle and hacking through bamboo. Their mission was scheduled to commence at first light.

Roberto had just checked his watch; it was 0200 and time to wake the next soldier due to stand guard. As he began to rise he spotted a lurking shadow just outside their perimeter. Before he could raise his AC556, the jungle night was ripped open at its seams and the sky came alive. A Viet Cong patrol showered his squad with deafening grenades and mortar fire. The accompanying staccato of the NVA's AK-47s ripped into the trees, raining leaves, bark, and splinters onto the sleep-deprived, fatigued squad. The 7.62 x 39 125-grain bullets repeatedly found their targets with the thud of impacted flesh followed by the last gasp of a dying soldier or unceasing cries for a medic. "Medic," God he hated that word. The ammo flashes were like thousands of fireflies deciding to be active at the same time. At 0230 the firefight was over, and the Nagoolians had disappeared into the night as quickly and silently as they had appeared. The only sounds remaining were the anguished cries of pain from the near mortally wounded men of his squad. By sunrise only two members of the assault force were still alive, Roberto and the medic, who sat holding the youngest member of their squad in his arms while attempting to sob away his feeling of total uselessness.

Roberto would never forget the mud- and blood-covered medic looking up at him and repeatedly saying, through gut- and chest-wrenching sobs, "I'm so sorry, Sarge. I'm so sorry."

Roberto always awoke covered in perspiration, yelling, "Medics, where the hell are you?" Slowly he got out of bed and made his way to the kitchen to pour ice-cold water over his head. It was the only way he'd found to make the pain and the agony of the night disappear. And the recurring nightmares were why he still traveled to Billings once a month for his post-traumatic stress disorder group therapy session at the VA Outpatient Clinic.

CHAPTER 2

The early morning sun's rays wafted through the curtainless bedroom window and silently stretched across the room, reaching for Roberto's face. Like soft, smooth fingers stroking his cheek, the warm sun awakened him. His first thought was that it had been a good night, no nightmares. His second was to just lie there and bask in the warmth of the sun. He occasionally imagined that this must be what it was like to be in an incubator. But he stretched, rolled out of bed, and headed for the kitchen to start a fresh pot of coffee.

He opened the door to let Bogey, his English bullmastiff, out before changing into his running gear. He tried to start every morning with a five-mile run on a trail he had carved through the woods, having convinced himself it was not only invigorating but healthy.

After a steaming hot shower and his first cup of coffee, Roberto thought about the day. He had to go into town again. It was the first Tuesday of the month, which meant it was time for his monthly visit to the VA Outpatient Clinic for his post-traumatic stress disorder group therapy session. Dr. Johnslin, his therapist, had been doing some cognitive behavioral therapy with him. He repeatedly referred to it as CBT and had told Roberto it was the current standard of care as established by the Department of Defense.

Supposedly, Roberto would learn to identify thoughts that made him feel afraid or upset and replace them with less distressing thoughts. It sounded like a bunch of psychological mumble jumble bullshit. He wasn't sure these sessions were beneficial, but it was a reason, or excuse—take your pick—to go to town. Besides, he enjoyed the company of most of the men in his group, and he wanted to pick up some new books at the library.

DR. TERRELL JOHNSLIN, whom the men affectionately referred to as TJ, walked into the therapy room. The group had named the room the "hat box," thinking TJ would screw their hats on correctly in this little box. TJ threw his long white coat on the small desk in the corner of the room. He walked to his chair and smiled. "Administrators would like to think that better medicine is practiced if I wear one of those long coats. I think they're okay as a place to put pens and to keep puke and urine off your clothes." He held up his hands. "That being said, good morning, gentlemen, and in case you haven't noticed, we have a new member in our group. I would like to introduce Jesse Martinson."

The same eight men had been in TJ's group for the past year and a half. The group slowly turned and looked at this intruder with tight lips and furrowed brows as if to say: "Who the hell do you think you are coming into this group?" None of them said a word.

Martinson sheepishly looked around the circle of men before standing with her hands clasped behind her back. She looked at TJ and took a deep breath. "Look, guys. I didn't ask to be here, and I want you to know if I had my choice I'd be someplace else. Don't ask me where, but rest assured it sure as hell wouldn't be with you jerk-offs. So, let's say you stuff your male egos in your back pockets, turn down your testosterone dials a notch, and let the good doc do his work. Having a woman in the group may actually help some of you get on with your lives." She nodded at TJ, who grinned, and sat down with her arms folded across her chest.

TJ looked around the room and his eyes locked on Roberto's. Finally, getting the doc's silent message, he coughed to clear his throat and gazed down at the floor for a second before standing. Roberto looked at the newest member of their group. "Pardon my friends for their lack of social skills. Welcome to group in the hat box." After glancing at the floor for a few seconds, he nodded and smiled. "You're right, you know. You being here just might help some of these jerk-offs, as you called them, get on with their lives." He looked at TJ, who coughed to cover up his smile

TJ nodded at Roberto. "Thank you, Mr. DeLaCroix, for your warm welcome." He looked at his newest patient. "Ms. Martinson, perhaps you would be so kind as to tell the group your story."

She slowly relaxed and put her forehead in her hands, kicking the floor. Chairs started shuffling. TJ held up his hands to quiet them. Ms. Martinson stood, wiped her eyes with the backs of her hand, kicked her chair over, and started circling the group.

One of the men, Cpl. Joey Beachman, looked at TJ as if to ask, "What the . . .?" TJ motioned for him to remain seated and wait. He started to stand and Roberto grabbed him by the thigh and gently pushed him back onto his chair. Roberto pointed at his watch and held up three fingers. "Give her three minutes. We did the same for you."

TJ said in his soft, calming voice, "Ms. Martinson, we're waiting for you."

She slowly returned to her chair and began her story. "I was assigned to a supply company in the Gulf War." Looking around the room, she smirked and continued. "Some of you young guys may remember it better as Operation Desert Storm." She looked down for a second before wiping away the tears streaming down her cheeks. "We were in a convoy hauling some supplies and, I have to admit, I was in a pissed off mood that day, so the driver had me sit next to the window. Said I was 'raggy' and he didn't want me too close. Said he didn't want my bad attitude to infect him. He was perhaps my best friend in the outfit. Anyway, he was killed when we were hit by what we were later told was friendly fire. And so was a young guy who was sitting in the back of the truck." She pounded her thigh with her fist. "Friendly fire my ass! What a bunch of bullshit!" She wiped more tears away with the backs of her hands. "Poor dumb luck kid in the back had only been with us for one week. I really didn't even know him." She gasped, then retrieved a tissue from the front pocket of her jeans and loudly blew her nose. "I was knocked unconscious and stayed that way for two days. They flew me to Frankfurt, where I was hospitalized for two weeks with a constant freaking worst-ever headache. I still get the headaches. And I still see the truck blowing up, and I have these nightmares of my friend being blown to bits, in slow motion, while looking at me with his hands out like he was asking me why I wasn't helping him."

She got up and paced back and forth before stopping and staring at TJ. "Then I began to develop this myriad of symptoms including fatigue, anxiety, and depression in addition to the continuing headaches." She glanced at the floor and looked around, shaking her head. "Felt so horseshit that a lot of days I couldn't even get my sorry ass out of bed. The psych docs told me that it's all probably PTSD. I've had a shitload of therapy over the years and enough pills to fill a box car." She nodded toward the group. "Now my docs think that you guys will help me overcome it, or at least learn how to deal with it." She sat down and raised her hands with a smile. "And that's my story."

The group was quiet for about thirty seconds before Sgt. Benjamin Lowell, a double amputee as the result of an IED, began to slowly clap. "Nice fricking story, Martinson. You're tired and have a headache, but look at me! I lost both legs!"

"Stuff it, Lowell!" Roberto said. "I've never met a sorrier asshole excuse for a man than you. Or, for that matter, anyone who feels sorrier for himself than you do. You've been sitting here for two years crying about life not being fair, but you haven't done one damn thing to make yours any better."

TJ spoke up. "Take it easy, Mr. DeLaCroix."

"I've told you before, Doc, please call me Roberto or Rob. Please don't call me Mr. and never call me Robbie."

Lowell sneered. "What's the matter, jungle man? Robbie make you feel like a little boy?"

Roberto leaped to his feet and grabbed Lowell by the neck. He pushed the wheelchair against the wall and stuck an index finger between Lowell's eyes. He spoke through jaws clenched so tightly he later wondered why he didn't break any teeth. "Look, you sand-snorting soldier wannabe, who's a little boy now?"

Lowell, choking and gasping for air, began to turn a light shade of purple while futilely pulling at Roberto's left hand. Roberto maintained his grip while thumping Lowell on the forehead with each word. "Never, repeat, never call me Robbie. Is that clear?"

TJ sprinted over and squeezed the muscles in Roberto's neck, causing his arm to ache and his grip to weaken. "Let him go, Rob. Now!"

Roberto released his grip and slowly stood while still staring at the coughing and gasping Lowell. He took a deep breath and looked at TJ. Roberto placed his hand on Lowell's shoulder. "Sorry, Ben. I don't know what came over me. I just don't like to be called Robbie. I've got my reasons, and it's not about being a little boy. Okay?"

"It's okay, Rob. It's just that when I heard her story it reminded me that I was driving a Humvee that hit an IED, killing my best friend, Staff Sergeant Joseph Jameson. You're absolutely right. I just haven't been able to move on. But I don't care what you say, it just ain't frickin' fair." He dropped his head into his hands and began to quietly weep.

TJ walked back to his chair and looked around the room. He knew it would be unorthodox, and perhaps even unprofessional, to end the session at such an emotional moment without exploring and resolving some of the feelings that had been triggered. But knowing these guys as he did, he didn't think there was anything to be gained as individuals or as a group by continuing. "Well, I think we've had enough excitement for one day. What's say we call it a wrap and pick it up again next month? Everyone okay with that?"

No one said anything. They just got up, returned their chairs to the wheeled chair rack, and left. Except for Roberto who was still facing the wall where he had pushed Ben.

When it was just the two of them, TJ broke the silence. "Still having some anger issues huh, Roberto?"

"Yeah, I guess so, Doc. But they're getting less. Don't worry. I won't let this shit happen again."

"If there's something you want to talk about, just let me know, okay?"

"Nah. Thanks anyway, but I'll be okay." Roberto took a deep breath, stuffed his hands in his jeans, and headed for the door.

CHAPTER 3

Exiting the building Roberto was vaguely aware that someone was leaning against the railing separating the sidewalk from the lawn. He still had his hands stuffed in his jeans and was silently chastising himself for his behavior when he heard someone call to him, "Hey, DeLaCroix."

He decided to ignore it despite the voice being female. Then she called again, "Hey, Roberto. Or should I call you Rob?" When he didn't respond, she said mockingly, "Or how about Robbie?"

He froze. He could feel his anger titer growing again and the hairs on the back of his neck becoming stiff. He took a deep breath. He recognized the newest member of their group. What was her name, Martinson? Noting that she was becoming a bit apprehensive, he said, "Martinson, right?"

She nodded.

"Look, I'm not going to throw you up against a wall and crush your larynx, but I meant it when I said I did not like being called Robbie. Got it?" He walked toward his truck.

"Hey, Rob. Would you like to get a cup of coffee? I'm buying."

Roberto stopped, took another deep breath, and shrugged. "Ah, what the hell, why not. The day can't get any worse. There's a nice coffee shop around the corner. Come on, and I'm buying, not you."

CHAPTER 4

Eddie took his eyes off the road for a second and glanced over at his friend Bobby. "Why'd ya do it, Bobby? Why'd ya shoot that poor old man?"

Bobby, slouched down in the seat and staring out the side window, was twirling a .22 caliber Smith and Wesson on his finger. He sat up and laid the pistol on the seat. "Why not, Eddie?" He rubbed his face with both hands and let out a low whistle. "You just don't get it, do you, Eddie? Do you think all the big guys started with their biggest heist? Do you think that painter… ah, ah, ah shit, screw his name, started with the Mona Lisa? No, dumb shit. They all started with small things just like we did. That's why I picked a small 7-11 for our first job."

Eddie gripped the steering wheel of the rusting light blue Suburban so tightly his fingers began turning white. He pounded his fist on the wheel with each word. "But why'd ya have to shoot the harmless old man? He gave us the money. What'd we get, twenty-five bucks? Now we got murder hanging on us, Dude."

Bobby sneered. "Now how was I to know? He was wearing that turban so low on his head. I was just going to put a hole through the towel. You know, make it easier for him to hang it up whenever he took it off. Now watch the road, Dude, or you'll miss our turn. I told you I cased this area and there's an old road up ahead on the right that leads into the foothills. We can hang out and lay low for a few days before heading south to Wyoming. Gotta be some easy grabs over there. Come on, Eddie. Don't go soft on me now. Trust me, things are going to blow over, and we'll be cool, Dude."

Bobby leaned forward and pointed to the right. "There, Dude. That's the road. Take it and slow down because it's rough."

"But what if someone lives here, Bobby? Then what're we gonna do, shoot him too?"

Bobby raised and lowered his hands in a soothing manner. "Eddie, Eddie, Eddie. I said trust me. I'll take care of everything. If the dude needs offing, well, what's one more? Now just watch where you're driving."

CHAPTER 5

Roberto turned into his driveway and stopped his dark blue F250 Ford pickup. He eased out of the door and waited for Bogey to follow. Roberto scratched Bogey's ears while surveying the entrance to his driveway. He walked forward and noted the busted monofilament line lying in each ditch. He had developed the habit of stringing a light green four-pound monofilament line across the driveway and securing it to a post in each ditch. Simple but effective, it was his security system. He bent down and picked up one end of the busted line. Twirling it in his fingers, he stared up the driveway. He scratched his best friend's ears again. "Well, Bogey, looks like we got us some company. Hope they don't plan on staying long." He turned back to his truck and gave Bogey an almost imperceptible signal to heel.

He started Big Blue and unhurriedly drove toward the house. About fifty yards from the driveway entrance, he had created a small clearing for just such situations. He parked in the clearing and Bogey bounded out after him. He took care not to slam the door. No sense giving his unexpected company any warning. Tucked into the thickets was a camouflage-painted metal box with a lock incapable of being busted by bullets or bolt cutters. He twirled the dial to his set combination, slid the lock from the hasp, and lifted the lid. Standing back, Roberto allowed a grin as he reviewed the contents. He slid his favorite KA-BAR knife into the space between his jeans and his belt. Then he held up a government-model M1911a1 Colt pistol for a quick inspection. He released the magazine and filled it with seven .45 ACP caliber bullets. He put one into the chamber and slammed the magazine into place. He filled two other magazines and slipped them in his right back pocket. He never stored the handgun or the magazines with bullets in them for fear of weakening the springs. He sure as hell didn't want a weak spring fail to throw a bullet into the chamber when he was staring down the barrel of a weapon held by some badass dude. After carefully wiping the pistol down on his sleeve, he tucked it between his pants and the small of his back.

The final weapon he thought he'd need for this mission was his reworked M16A1. He lifted it and a couple of magazines from its storage place. He slammed one mag into place before looking down the sight line. He stuffed the other mag in his left rear pocket and then slung the rifle over his shoulder.

He locked the storage box and leaned down to scratch Bogey's ears. "Well, Boy, let's go greet our visitors." He stiffened slightly and tilted his head to the north thinking he could hear something. There it was, the sound of sirens coming his way. Kneeling, he took Bogey's huge head in both hands. "Seems like our visitors may have caused some people to be upset. Well, we'll just have to be a bit more careful than normal." He stood, gave Bogey the heel signal, and started through the brush.

He knew every rock, bush, and tree on this property. He also knew all the game trails and picked up one heading toward his house. Easing his way along the trail, he recalled the painstaking care he had employed when he built his log home. It wasn't much, but it was more than enough for him and had taken almost a year to complete. He had veered from his initial plan and had electricity put in. The work was good therapy and left him so fatigued at the end of the day that the nightmares were rare. Life in his mountain world was good, and he was not about to let some uninvited intruders destroy it.

The game trail came within fifty feet of the small clearing where Roberto had constructed his home. Standing quietly, he surveyed the area and noted a rusted-out old light blue Suburban next to his house. But he didn't see any people. The questions came: how many, how old, are they armed, what did they do and why did they have to pick his place? Well, no matter, he'd just have to deal with it. He eased through the brush to the edge of the clearing, allowing a clear view of the door on the east side of the cabin. Kneeling down, he instinctively began scratching Bogey's ears. "Stay here, Bogey. I'll call you when I need you."

He eased back into the brush and started circling around to the west. The area he'd cleared to construct his home was about fifty yards in diameter. The rest was thick, almost impenetrable brush interspersed with large white pine. It made the cover for his trek excellent, but he was sustaining numerous scratches on his hands and face. After ten minutes, half of which was spent on his hands and knees, he had a good view of the west side of his house. Through the two dust-covered windows, he could see two young men in the kitchen, and one was obviously quite agitated.

Using the sun at his back to his advantage, he hunched down and crept up to the space between the windows separating the kitchen from his bedroom. He eased himself up, keeping his back to the wall, removed his tattered cap, and turned to look inside. An agitated young man was pacing the room while running his hands through his long greasy hair. He stopped pacing and pointed at his seemingly untroubled accomplice, who was slouched in Roberto's soft overstuffed leather chair with one leg draped over the armrest. Roberto noticed that the intruder had the balls to take one of his beers.

He slid back down the wall and crept around to the east side, emitting a soft whistle to summon Bogey. When he reached the entrance door, he knelt down and began his routine of scratching Bogey's ears. Lifting an index finger he said, "Stay. Guard."

He put his ear to the door and heard the agitated one yelling, "Jeez, Bobby! Just tell me something. Anything! What's our plan? I'm scared as hell, and I want to know just what the hell we're going to do!" Before the slouched one could respond, Roberto stood, straightened his jacket, leaned the M16A1 against the doorjamb, and opened the door.

"Welcome to my home, young fellas. What brings you all the way out here? You're obviously not Jehovahs, and I'm not the kind of guy who would want to buy any encyclopedias or brushes."

Scraggly Hair stopped pacing and, were it not for the situation, he would have been comical. His mouth gaped open, revealing his teeth to be as unkempt as his hair, and his knees looked like they were going to buckle. A quick glance convinced Roberto the young ingrate had not wet himself, at least not yet. The sloucher sat frozen, but dropped the beer. Roberto's immediate thought was now he'd have to clean up that mess as well.

"I see you found my beer. I hope you had the courtesy to at least save one for me. Now, one more time, ladies, what are you doing in my home?"

Roberto saw the slight movement of sloucher's right hand as he reached for the space between his leg and the chair. "I just wouldn't do that if I were you, Son. You reach any further and you'll be dead before you can touch that piece." He nodded at Scraggly Hair. "I suggest you sit before you fall over. Just a reminder, you shit or piss your pants and get any on my floor, I'm going to clean it up with that twisted, greasy mat on top of your ugly head. Now grab a chair and pull it up next to your wannabe buddy over there."

He turned his attention back to the sloucher. "The first thing I want you to do, Jesse James, is to sit up straight. Then stand and pick up your piece with your teeth and drop it on the floor." The sloucher just stared at him until Roberto yelled, "Move!" He slowly stood, cocked his head to the side, and through a sneer said, "You want it, come and get it, Asshole."

Roberto reached behind him and opened the door. "Bogey, here."

The two-hundred-pound slobbering bullmastiff rushed to Roberto's side. Upon seeing the intruders, he stiffened, bared his teeth, and emitted a low growl. He looked like he'd enjoy nothing more than ripping them apart, and the sight was apparently enough to make a believer of the sloucher. He raised his hands and, although pale, he retained his cocky sneer. "Okay, Dude. Just hold off old Scooby Doo there, okay?"

"His name is Bogey and you have thirty seconds to pick up that pistol with your teeth or you'll get to know him quite well."

A quick glance toward Scraggly Hair confirmed one of Roberto's fears. The punk had wet himself.

The sloucher picked up the .22 caliber Smith and Wesson with his teeth and stood staring at Roberto. Roberto nodded to the table. "Place it on the table, pull up another chair from the kitchen, and then sit your sorry ass down next to Wet Pants."

Roberto turned the chairs back to back, retrieved a roll of duct tape, and secured the uninvited guests. Knowing the one called Bobby was the leader, he faced him. "Okay, before I call the sheriff, why don't you tell me what you've done and what the hell you're doing here."

Bobby's gaze remained on the floor. Roberto kicked the chair. "Talk!" That prompted Bogey to ease forward and issue another throaty growl. Bobby raised his head and stared at Roberto with a look of intense hatred. He nonchalantly spit on the floor at Roberto's feet. "Go screw yourself, Mountain

Man. My old man's an attorney, and he will hand you your ass in a hand basket for the way you're treating us." He leaned back. "Eddie, don't you say one word! Got it? You know my old man will get us out of this."

Roberto kicked the chairs onto their sides causing both young men to cry out in surprise and pain.

"What the hell are you doing, you crazy idiot!" Bobby yelled.

Eddie was now crying. Roberto knelt on the floor and looked directly into Eddie's eyes. "How about you, Son, you want to tell me what's going on?"

Eddie began sobbing uncontrollably. His eyes were wide, red, and full of panic. Through gasps he said, "It was all Bobby's idea. He said it would be easy cash and no one would get hurt."

Bobby jerked the chair. "Shut up you stupid, gutless idiot! Don't tell this frickin' mountain man anything."

"I didn't want to do it, but he talked me into it. Can I go home now, Sir?"

"You worthless piece of scumbag shit! I should have known better than to count on you!"

Roberto spun the chairs around so he was facing Bobby. "Look, Asshole. Why don't you just shut up. I really don't want to have Bogey babysit you. The last time he did that, well, let's just say it wasn't pretty." He spun the chairs again and placed a hand on Eddie's shoulder. "Sorry, Son, but I don't think that's possible. I have a hunch you two did something to really upset some people. I'm going to cut the tape on you, however, and let you sit up. But your teenage wonder boyfriend…" He spun the chairs again. "Will stay where he is. Got that, Bobby?"

He gave the chairs another spin and cut the tape holding Eddie, who rubbed his wrists and right shoulder as he stood. Roberto just watched this scared, misdirected young man as he looked around and then sat on another chair, placing his hands in his lap in an obvious attempt to cover the wet area.

Roberto dialed the sheriff's office in Billings, and after a brief discussion he turned to his guests. "Well, kids, now we wait for the sheriff to come and get you."

CHAPTER 6

A deputy sheriff arrived within an hour to take Yellowstone County's two newest felons into custody. Bobby was slouched over and mumbling about what his dad was going to do while being led away. And Eddie was still tearful and obviously mindful of his wet pants as he followed Bobby.

Roberto grabbed one of the remaining cold beers and sat in front of his fireplace with Bogey lying on the floor next to him. He stared at the fireplace, thinking that each of the leaping flames born among the logs, bright, hot and intense, represented his life. As each flame rose higher and traveled further on its life path, it became narrower, less bright and less intense, until it died out. Just that fast. And all that remained was some dull ash.

He was attempting to determine exactly where on his life's path he was when he realized he had finished his beer. He became cognizant of the deafening quiet, except for the crackling of the logs as they submitted to the unending hunger of the fire. Why had he reacted the way he did when Ben Lowell, who really wasn't that bad of a guy, called him Robbie? What did that mean?

He got up from his chair and went over to the old roll top desk in the corner of the room. He removed the key from the top drawer and unlocked the lower right hand drawer. There was only one item in the drawer, an old letter. He grabbed another beer out of the refrigerator, popped it open, and took a long pull from the can on his way back to his chair. He scratched Bogey's ears. "What do you think, old partner? Should I read this thing again? Ah, what the hell. That's why I got it out, right?"

Bogey's response was to use his hind leg to scratch his own ear and then settle in next to his master's chair.

Roberto took another long pull from the can of beer before opening the letter for, he guessed, the umpteenth time.

My dearest Robbie,

This is the hardest, most difficult thing I have ever done. By now you've probably guessed what this letter is about. It just can't be between us Robbie. Not like we thought it would be when we were in high school. You were just the most sweetest, gentlest, kindest man I had ever met. Remember those nights we sat in your dad's car down by the crick and just looked at the stars and talked? Remember all the plans we made and how we talked about how the world would be ours someday? And then you went into that damn Army. Pardon my French, but the Army really changed you, Robbie. Even before you went to Viet Nam to fight that stupid war. You were already different when you came home from your basic training. Sometimes you even scared me. But I really thought, and prayed that things would be different and be like they were before. But when you came home from your first tour in Viet Nam my greatest fears came true. You were not the Robbie DeLaCroix I had fallen in love with. And I could tell you were not going to change. Especially since you signed up to go back. Why, oh God why did you ever do that to yourself? And to us? Do you know how many nights I cried myself to sleep over you? Well, I'm not angry anymore Robbie. But I am sad. I'm sad for you. I've found another man, Robbie. Someone who is soft and kind and gentle and treats me right. I hope you find whatever it is you're looking for Robbie. I will always have a spot for you in my heart.

Take care and please don't get killed over there,

Lori Lynn

After he read it for the second time, he refolded it, returned it to the yellowing, frail envelope, and locked it in the same desk drawer. He grabbed another beer and returned to his chair. Reaching down to scratch Bogey's ears again, he said to his best friend, "Well, at least it gets a little easier each time I read it. Who knows, maybe someday I'll read it and laugh. The question is, will I ever find whatever it is I'm supposedly looking for?"

He opened the beer and took a long drink. This Martinson lady was kind of nice. Maybe they'd have coffee again another time.

CHAPTER 7

Norb "Nube" Lawson sat in his Billings, Montana, office and remembered the day he'd sat on a bench in front of the main entrance to the J. Edgar Hoover Building, at 935 Pennsylvania Avenue NW, and said to himself, *Washington, D.C.,—you either love it...or you hate it.* And he still wasn't sure where he stood on that question. It had been exactly five months and four days since he had returned to Washington, D.C., to resume his career with the FBI. Prior to that he had been in Oak Ridge, Minnesota, on what was officially listed as a bereavement leave after his wife Ellie was tragically killed in a motor vehicle accident.

During his stay in Oak Ridge, he had been asked to participate in the investigation of the brutal murders of two teenagers. But the investigation was complicated when Nube met Nancy Jameson, an Iraq war widow, and her young son Peter James, who preferred to be called PJ. The feelings he had developed for Nancy was not something he had counted on happening. His life was further complicated when his boss, Supervisory Special Agent Alessandra Corrales, called Nube and told him that he had to either return and resume his career or resign.

With his feet propped up on his desk, he recalled sitting on that bench watching the last remnants of a late winter snow succumbing to the warming rays of the early morning sun. He also recalled the angst he felt prior to the meeting with Corrales later that spring day when he had to give her his answer about whether or not he wanted to accept another assignment. Since his return to the bureau, he had actually enjoyed his work. But it was clouded by the nagging ache in his heart.

He stared out the window of his Billings office. He realized he'd been totally oblivious to the bright sun washing through the dust-covered window and slowly making its way up his outstretched legs. He also recalled how painful it had been to tell Nancy he was returning to Washington, D.C., to resume his FBI career. They had promised to stay in touch and to visit. Initially he called her two to three times a week, but lately it was just once a week. And the calls were becoming shorter. He did enjoy, however, the opportunity to chat with PJ and found he really missed that little boy. He smiled as he thought about the trip he was planning to visit the Jamesons in October.

He dropped his feet to the floor, ran his fingers through his hair, and looked at the mess on his desk. He may be in the Billings office of the Salt Lake City division of the FBI, but he was busy. Criminals, like illness, take no holidays and always provide more than enough work.

CHAPTER 8

Benno Donnrud had met Lloyd Malin while they were cellmates in the Wasatch medium security house in the Utah State Penitentiary in Draper, Utah. Both had been sentenced five years: Lloyd for assault with intent to do great bodily harm without murder and Benno for unarmed robbery and resisting arrest. Benno knew Lloyd was a crazy son of a bitch, but he was the first real friend he'd ever had. They spent too many sleepless nights talking about how the system had screwed them and how they were going to make it big when they got out of the big house. But Benno also realized Lloyd was a loose cannon.

Sitting in their dingy room in the Lucky Night motel, which advertised rates per hour rather than by the day or week, Benno tried to take stock of his situation. The two chairs were covered with torn red vinyl. Neither of the beds had been made in a week, and the mattresses were so bad the only place you could sleep was in the middle.

He took a deep breath of the room's air, an amalgamation of musky body odor and remnants of stale beer in the dozen or so cans strewn about the room. Added to this was a hint of pepperoni emanating from the scattered cardboard pizza boxes and the nauseating odor of the remnants of too many Marlboros overflowing three ashtrays. The sights and smells of this new prison cell were harsh reminders that life right now was really shitty.

But if their plan worked, and he knew it would because Lloyd said it would, they would be rich real soon. Then he'd dump Lloyd and get a new ride, perhaps one of them Beamer convertibles or a new Lincoln pickup. The thought of Lincoln making a pickup was so foreign to him that he just shook his head and wondered what the hell else he'd see. Maybe next would be Cadillac making a pickup. That thought made him snicker, causing Lloyd to glance his way.

Anyway, when this job was done, he'd get a new ride, dump Lloyd, find himself a good woman, and enjoy life, maybe even go on a cruise. But first they had to pull off this job. He looked up from the plans he had been staring at. "Lloyd." With no response from his partner, he said in a louder, commanding voice, "Lloyd!"

This time Lloyd lifted his eyes from the fingernail he was picking at, shrugged, and sneered. "What the fu—"

Benno clasped his hands over his ears before Lloyd could finish the word. "Nooo! Don't say that word! I told you I hate that word! It's the only word my old man seemed to know, and you promised me in the pen you wouldn't say it. Jesus, Lloyd, don't you remember? You promised."

Lloyd raised his arms and snickered. "Yeah, yeah, yeah. Calm down, Little Man, before you get your shorts all tied in a bunch. Now, like I was saying, what you want that I can't finish my own manicure?"

"You want to go over the plans again? Maybe just one more time just to make sure?"

"Really? You want to go over the plans again." Benno hated it when Lloyd talked to him like this, real slow like he was a dumb ass. The muscles in Lloyd's neck, around his tarantula tattoo, twitched. Lloyd lifted his right lip a bit which was as close to a smile as he ever got. "Benno, my main man. Don't be so damn hyper. Things are cool."

Benno flicked his wrist. "And will you please turn so I don't see that frickin' spider? I told you it freaks me out!" Lloyd had told him he got the tattoo because he thought it was cool, and when his neck twitched, it made the tarantula look like it was alive and crawling. He thought it drove the chicks crazy, but Benno was positive it just proved how psycho the nut case was and all the more reason to dump him right after this job.

"And I told you it's not a spider. It's a tarantula and I won't turn away. And I don't wanna look at the plans again. We've been over them a gazillion times, and I've got it. So just relax." He raised his brow and cocked his head as if to say, "Okay?" With that he returned his attention to his manicure.

Keeping his finger on the map in front of him, Benno shook his head. Stupid ass Lloyd with his military-like hair cut on top and the long mullet hanging down to his shoulders. And if anyone took a close look at him, they'd know he was a con with that prison weightlifting junkie body. All muscle in his arms and upper body and skinny legs. He always wondered why those stupid assholes never worked on their legs.

He returned his gaze to the cheap WalMart-special card table where he had taped a hand-drawn map. He leaned forward, placing both hands on the table. Squinting, he thought that as soon as they pulled off this job he was going to buy himself some reading glasses. He tapped the red circle drawn around the corner of Third Street and Buckman Avenue. This was the home of Moskowitz Jewelers.

They knew from their surveillance that the armored car arrived promptly every Thursday at 0900. The driver, a mustachioed overweight man in his mid-sixties, was probably staring retirement right in the face. He always stayed in the truck, opened a candy bar, and began reading the paper. His partner was a well-buffed macho type, who appeared to be in his mid-thirties, who Benno thought took his job way too seriously. He would exit the vehicle, do a thirty-second survey of the street, then retrieve the cash bag from Moskowitz's and take it to the rear door of the truck. He always knocked twice on the door, and it was usually about ten to fifteen seconds before a thin bespectacled man of around fifty opened the door and received the bag. Based on Benno and Lloyd's surveillance, the time it took for the man to exit the store and pass the bag to the man in the rear of the truck was about twenty-five to thirty-five seconds. That was the window for Benno and Lloyd.

The plan called for Benno and Lloyd, disguised as priests, to intercept the guard just as he exited the jewelry store. Lloyd would spray the guard's face with pepper spray while Benno grabbed the cash bag. They would use the 2000 Ford Windstar van, which would be parked across the street, as their getaway vehicle. Benno figured thirty to forty seconds max to grab the bag and get to the van.

Benno traced the route down Buckman to 10th street he had meticulously drawn on the map. Here they would change vehicles and take the waiting black 1998 Jeep Cherokee and hop onto Highway 212 and head for Wyoming and the good life. Lloyd thought a good place to head for was Jackson Hole. So simple and no one would get hurt. Besides, Lloyd said that old man Moskowitz would have insurance and it wouldn't be any skin off their noses. Smiling, Benno nodded in silent agreement with himself, then opened the cooler and pulled the tab on another beer. It would help him relax and sleep. The smile grew as he thought, *Tomorrow is the big day.*

CHAPTER 9

This was a special day for Rabbi Ira Jacobson. He had been asked by Irving Moskowitz, the owner of Moskowitz Jewelers, to hang a mezuzah on the doorpost of his newly opened jewelry store. Although he had been the rabbi at the Temple Beth El Synagogue for the past three years, he had yet to preside over a mezuzah ceremony for a business. Rabbi Jacobson had spent two hours last week with Mr. Moskowitz and his wife Fredda, reviewing the ceremony they had scheduled for 9:00 a.m. today. During their meeting he had reminded Mr. and Mrs. Moskowitz that they were required to inscribe the words of the Shema on the doorpost of their business. He went on to explain to them that simply affixing a mezuzah to the doorframe would fulfill that mitzvah or Biblical commandment. The kosher parchment scroll prepared by the synagogue's sofer stam, or scribe, had been inserted into a decorative case chosen by Fredda Moskowitz and then placed in the briefcase Rabbi Jacobson was toting. He was intently reviewing the Likbo'a Mezuzah blessing as he turned the corner onto Buckman Avenue.

Irving Moskowitz stood on the sidewalk facing his store, with his head tilted, pointing absently at something on the right doorframe.

"Good morning, Mr. Moskowitz. I must say, you look like you're preoccupied with something serious."

"Oh, Rabbi Jacobson. Pardon me, but I didn't see or hear you coming. I'm just trying to decide where the best place would be to affix the mezuzah."

"You know, Irving, that we place it on the right side of the door, in the upper third of the doorpost, pointing upward and to the inside of the building."

"Yes, I know, Rabbi. However, I'm concerned about vandals. I don't want it stolen or destroyed." He shook his head. "There's so much of that going on lately."

"It's so sad when we have to think of those things, but I suppose you are correct." Ira Jacobson nodded. "I think God will understand if we hang it just a bit higher." Quietly, he added, "I guess we'll just have to think of this as theology, once again, bending to the chaos of today's undereducated and confused society."

While they each quietly pondered this from their own viewpoints, the Johansson Brothers armored truck pulled up to the curb. Ira smiled and nodded to the man who stepped out. The muscular young man politely nodded in return, surveying the street. He walked to the corner and glanced down Third Street before entering the store.

BENNO AND LLOYD HAD parked the Windstar van across the street from Moskowitz Jewelers at eight that morning. After a cup of what they deemed lousy coffee at Jill's Coffee and Cookie on the corner of 2nd and Buckman, they walked halfway down the block to the alleyway, where they changed into their costumes designed to make them look like priests. Standing behind the dumpster, Benno peered at the garbage scattered on the ground. Garbage was strewn around the alley, graffiti had been painted on the decaying brick walls, and unpainted, broken doors led into businesses on either side of the alley. For a moment he wondered if this reflected his life, a piece of unwanted, scattered garbage trying to find a home in the alley of life. *Ah shit, what the hell am I thinking about? Things are going to be great right after this job. Lloyd says so.*

Benno, trying to ease the tension he was feeling, looked over at Lloyd, who was fidgeting while trying to adjust his white clerical collar and straighten his fake beard. Benno began to laugh. "You look like shit, Lloyd. Anybody think you look like any priest is nuts."

Lloyd took the Marlboro out of his mouth, spit on the ground, and then took one last drag before throwing the butt on the cracked asphalt and grinding it out with his heel. "Yeah, well, you don't look like no religious guru yourself, Asshole." He chuckled. "Yeah, that would be a good name for you. Father Asshole."

Lloyd looked at his Mickey Mouse watch. He tapped the face and looked at his partner. "Should be here any time, Benno. You got your shit together? You going to be okay or are you going to piss your pants when the going gets hot?"

Fidgeting, Benno tugged at his fake beard. "You don't worry about me, Lloyd. I'll handle my part." He pointed at Lloyd's neck. "Don't you think you oughta try and cover up that spider? Jeez, it sticks out like a sore-ass thumb. Why don't you just hang a sign from your freakin' neck that says you're Lloyd Malin, famous armored car bandit?"

Lloyd stared at Benno through narrowed eyelids for a few seconds. Then he got right in his face and tapped his chest. "I told you it's a tarantula, got it? Don't you worry none about my tattoo. Just think about what we're gonna do, got it?"

An armored truck with "Johansson Brothers" painted on it in bold black letters passed the alleyway. "Okay, shit for brains," Lloyd said. "It's show time. Let's go."

They exited the alleyway and turned right to begin the half-block walk to Moskowitz Jewelers. Both men were tugging at their fake beards to make sure they were on properly. Lloyd had become conscious of his tattoo after Benno's inane comment, and he tried to pull his jacket up while pulling his neck down, somewhat turtle-like.

About halfway to the end of the block, Lloyd saw the two men standing in front of the building housing Moskowitz Jewelers. One of the men appeared to be a rabbi. Benno grabbed Lloyd's arm and, turning to him, almost stumbled. "Lloyd, look! One of those guys is a real rabbi! Now what the hell are we gonna do?"

Lloyd pulled his arm away from Benno's grasp and was about to say something when a lady ran up behind them. "Fathers! Fathers! Please wait! I need to ask you something!" The lady, obviously short of breath, grabbed each man by the arm. She released Benno's arm as she put her hand on her chest, trying to catch her breath. "Oh, Fathers, thank you for stopping. I just came out of Jill's and happened to see the two of you, and I have to ask you something. Will there be a Mass tonight at St. Mark's? I feel so bad that I missed Mass this past Sunday and want to go tonight—to make it up, you know—and St. Mark's is the closest Catholic church. And I just feel so blessed that I happened to see you. Will there be Mass tonight?"

Lloyd glanced at the armored truck and knew their time was short. Benno was nervously bouncing from one foot to the other. Lloyd looked back at the lady and pulled his arm away. He gave her a slight push and said, with the coldest voice he could muster, "Look, Lady. We ain't no freakin' priests. So just get lost. Get the hell outta here, got it?"

He grabbed Benno. "Let's go, Asshole. Time's a wasting. That dude will be out of the building in a few seconds."

They turned from the lady and began the last few steps to the end of the block. However, she was persistent. "There must be some mistake. I know I've seen you two at St. Mark's."

She was still tugging at their arms, with both men trying to shake her loose, when the door to Moskowitz Jewelers opened and the young, buff, armored car employee stepped out onto the sidewalk holding the moneybag. Lloyd was reaching inside his jacket for the can of pepper spray when the frustrated lady put her hands on her hips. She yelled at the two impostors, "Why won't you give me an answer? It's just a simple question!"

Lloyd abruptly turned to her with the pepper spray in his hand. "Look, you dumb bitch. I told you we ain't no frickin' priests!" And with that he shot some pepper spray toward her face.

Benno grabbed Lloyd by the arm. He was now in a state of panic. "What the hell you doin', Lloyd? Spray the guard! Now!"

The guard yelled at his partners in the truck, "Start the truck and get her moving!"

IRVING MOSKOWITZ, STARTLED OUT OF HIS state of contemplation, grabbed at his chest and began gasping for air. Small beads of perspiration developed on his forehead and the color left his face, leaving him with a ghost-like pallor. He reached for the sleeve of Rabbi Jacobson's coat as he slumped to the ground.

Rabbi Jacobson, still mulling over the latest insult to theology he had been discussing with Irving, allowed himself to be pulled down by the weight of the sagging jeweler. He gestured to the impostors. "What is the meaning of this? Can't you see what you've done to poor Mr. Moskowitz? We need to call an ambulance immediately!"

Lloyd glanced at the rabbi. "Shut up, Preacher Man, and you won't get hurt." He whirled around and began spraying the pepper spray in the direction of the guard, who had dropped into a defensive position and was trying to free his .357 Smith and Wesson from his holster. Lloyd dropped to one knee, affording him a direct shot at the guard, and gave him another quick spray. Then he threw the can at him, reached into his coat pocket, and retrieved a Ruger .38 caliber pistol. Falling to his left, he squeezed off two quick shots at the guard, who fell onto his back grabbing his chest.

Lloyd rose quickly and grabbed the moneybag. Turning to Benno he shouted, "Grab the broad! We might need a hostage!" He pointed the handgun at the rabbi. "On your feet, Prayer Man! You're comin' with us!"

Ira Jacobson, who was now on his knees and praying over his gasping friend, looked up and spoke in a quiet, calm voice. "I will not leave my friend, and I implore you once again to please call an ambulance."

Lloyd grabbed him by the right shoulder. Lifting the rabbi nearly off his feet, he glared at him and spoke through clenched teeth. "I said get your ass up and come with me! Now!"

Ira, assaulted by fetid cigarette breath and the look of sheer terror in the eyes of his assailant, turned once again to his fallen friend. But before he could say anything, he felt himself being dragged, stumbling, out into the street.

His assailant's companion stared with mouth agape. "Lloyd, what the hell did you do? We said no one gets hurt. And no guns!"

The man called Lloyd stood in front of the armored vehicle. The driver was talking into his radio. Lloyd fired off two quick shots at the windshield, shattering it. The shot created a starburst effect. Lloyd pointed the pistol at his sidekick. "I said grab the broad and get your ass moving! Now! Or the next two are for you!"

Benno grasped the startled, crying lady, who held both hands over her mouth. "You heard the man, Lady! Let's go!" She didn't move so he pulled her so hard she almost fell. Benno started to run and the lady stumbled. He strengthened his grip and held her up. "I'm sorry, Lady. I promise you that you won't get hurt!" He got a quick glimpse of the wounded guard still on the ground, but at least he was moving. The jeweler, however, looked like he was one bad-off dude.

By the time Benno reached the middle of the street, Lloyd had the side door of the van open and was in the driver's seat with the motor running. Benno pushed their unwilling companion into the van, jumped in behind her, and pulled the door closed while Lloyd was already accelerating away from the curb. Benno's last view was of the armored vehicle's driver exiting the truck with his pistol drawn. He heard the two slugs pound into the rear door of the van before he heard the loud, explosive noise of the discharged side arm.

Lloyd threw the .38 handgun into the back. "Hold the gun on them, and if they try anything, shoot 'em. Got it?"

Benno fumbled to pick up the weapon. He pointed it in the direction of the two unsuspecting victims. "What the hell did you just do back there, Lloyd? You said it would be easy, that no one would get hurt, and we had agreed that we wouldn't use any guns! And we kidnapped two people! Do you have any idea what the hell that means? Or have you gone completely nuts?"

He knew, just as he said it, that he should never have questioned his partner's sanity. Before Benno could say anything else, he felt the sting of the backhand Lloyd delivered to his face. Lloyd glared at him in the rearview mirror, "Look, you little godforsaken weasel, I run this show, not you. And if I think we need to use guns, we use 'em. Got it? And, who knows, we might need these two as bargaining chips."

CHAPTER 10

Roberto liked his neighbor. Old Clyde Ashburn, an eighty-two-year-old widower, was a retired forest ranger who lived a mile south of him in a small log cabin not unlike Roberto's. He had moved into his home shortly after his wife of forty-six years passed away from complications of congestive heart failure. Clyde rarely left his place, so Roberto usually checked with him when he was headed to town just in case Clyde needed something. Clyde told Roberto that he was running short on some of his medications and would appreciate it if he would pick some up for him at the South Billings Target pharmacy.

After finding some Ibuprofen for himself, Roberto walked to the counter to hand Clyde's empty prescription bottles to the pharmacist. A sniffling, agitated young man brushed past him and confronted the pharmacist. He wiped his nose with his sleeve as he lifted a small handgun in his trembling hand. He stuttered when he spoke. "I want you to give me your cash and your OxyContin! Now! And, and don't make me shoot you!" He pointed the gun at the pharmacist. "Hurry, Mister! I don't have all day and like I said, I don't want to have to shoot you!"

Roberto shook his head. *Shit. Here we go again.* "You don't want to do this, Son. Just put the gun away and walk out of here."

The young man's eyes were bloodshot, his pupils were pinpoints, and there were beads of perspiration on his forehead. He pointed the pistol at Roberto with a trembling hand. "Butt out, Old Man."

He swung the gun toward the pharmacist again. "Hurry up with the cash and the oxy! Don't make me shoot you! I will you know!"

"Look, Son…" Roberto tried again. "I mean it. You don't want to do this. Just put the piece away and walk out of here and no one gets hurt."

The young man stumbled as he swung around and pointed the gun at Roberto's face. "I said butt out, Old Man! Or I'll shoot you too!"

Roberto turned his palms toward the young assailant and smiled. "Son, I'll give you just one more chance to put that thing away and get out of here. As a matter of fact, I will give you just ten seconds, and then I'm going to make you wish you had stayed in bed today. Or at home with your lousy supply of whatever the hell you're smoking and shooting. Got it?"

The young man raised the pistol higher and opened his mouth as if to utter another threat. Roberto sensed his desperation and fear. He ducked under the junkie's outstretched arm and, in the same motion, grabbed his gun hand and twisted it, causing the young man to lose his grip on the handgun. At the same time Roberto drove the heel of his right hand into the perpetrator's solar plexus, causing him to double over gasping for air. He stumbled and, still gasping, vomited profusely. Roberto released his grip on the addict's hand and let him fall into his vomitus. The immobilization of this young antagonist had taken less than three seconds.

As the young man lay on the floor, gasping and holding his abdomen, Roberto calmly kicked the pistol to the side. He looked at the pharmacist. "Better call an ambulance and the police."

The stunned pharmacist stood with mouth agape, failing to move. Roberto put on a hint of a smile. "Don't worry.

He's going to be okay. I didn't hurt him too bad. Just prevented a young, mixed-up kid from doing something really dumb. Now, please make those calls. And, by the way, I need you to refill a couple of prescriptions for Clyde Ashburn."

The police and the ambulance arrived at about the same time. A quick assessment by the EMTs proved Roberto correct. The young malefactor would need some medical attention, but he would be okay.

The detective who responded to the call, Detective Second-Grade Jonathan Lindsberg, asked the usual questions and, after being assured by the pharmacist that Roberto had acted in self-defense, asked Roberto to come down to the local precinct to give his statement before being released. As Roberto was leaving with the detective, the pharmacist called out to him, "Hey, Sir. Thanks for your help, and Clyde's prescriptions will be ready when you return."

CHAPTER 11

Lloyd swerved down Buckman Avenue, sideswiping two cars leaving their parking spaces. He was half turned in his seat because he did not entirely trust Benno. And he was trying to get out of the idiotic priest costume. Why the hell did he ever listen to Benno when he suggested this stupid disguise? When he careened off the second car, a silver VW Jetta, Benno yelled at him. "Jeez, Lloyd! Look where the hell you're goin'! Are you trying to get us killed before the cops catch us and do it for us?"

"Benno, you just shut your pie hole and keep that gun on the broad and the preacher man. If they attempt to even move and you don't shoot them, so help me God, I will shoot you. And try to get that stupid broad to quit her yelling and crying before I shut her up."

The rabbi, who was sitting calmly in the third seat of the van, was trying to calm the other unfortunate victim of this fiasco. He stopped patting her shoulder and looked at the driver in the rearview mirror. "Do what you must with yourself and your partner and take me if you feel you need a hostage, but I ask you, in God's name, to free this poor lady. Can't you see what you're doing to her?"

Benno held the gun up in his trembling hand. "Preacher Man, if I were you I would just shut up." He nodded toward his partner. "Maybe I can't, but Lloyd won't have a problem shooting you."

Lloyd pulled into the parking spot behind the Jeep they had parked earlier this morning and hit the brakes. However, because of his speed, he ran into the back of the waiting Cherokee, causing all of them to lurch forward. Lloyd struck his chest on the steering wheel, and the other three fell into the space between the seats. Lloyd had the momentary thought that he was glad the air bag didn't deploy. He yelled at Benno. "Get outta the van and bring those two with you! I'm going to torch this thing!"

"Just leave the damn van, Lloyd. If you torch it the cops will know where we left it. Let's just get the hell outta here."

"I'm going to get rid of the prints and these monkey suits. Saw it in a movie once."

"Don't you think you left your prints back there on the spray can, you idiot?"

"Benno, I swear, you call me an idiot once more and I'll kill you with my bare hands. Now grab the broad and the preacher man and let's move!"

Lloyd threw the door of the van open and jumped out, carrying the moneybag. Benno struggled to right himself and waved the pistol at the two captives. "You heard what Lloyd said, move it, come on!" He pushed the door of the van open, grabbed the screaming lady, and pointed the weapon at the rabbi. "Come on, get the hell outta there!"

Folding his arms over his chest, the rabbi spoke calmly. "I'm not moving, Son."

Hearing the Jeep roar to life, Benno panicked and fired a shot over the rabbi's head. The bullet grazed his hat and lodged in the roof of the van. "I mean it! Get the hell outta there! Now!"

The rabbi's lips began to move in silent prayer as he struggled to free himself from the rear seat. Benno ran up to the side of the Jeep, essentially dragging the sobbing lady with him. He pulled open the rear door and pushed her in. Waving the pistol at the rabbi, Benno yelled at him to get in the front seat.

Lloyd had the Jeep exiting the parking space before the rabbi had closed the door. Lloyd suddenly hit the brakes, squealing the Cherokee to a stop, turned, and backhanded the lady. He aimed his index finger at her as if he were aiming a pistol. "Now for the last time, Bitch. Shut the hell up or I will shut you up forever." He sneered. "Who knows, if you're good, and you behave, we may even let you go." The tires squealed as he headed down Buckman Avenue toward the entrance to Highway 212 South for Wyoming and the good life.

CHAPTER 12

Lloyd took a second to steal a glimpse at the speedometer when he hit Highway 212 South. He smiled when he saw the old Jeep was doing eighty miles per hour. He glanced in the rearview mirror and saw Benno looking at the floor and holding the pistol in his trembling right hand while running his left hand through his greasy hair. "Benno, Benno, Benno. Chill out, Dude. I told you we'd do this thing."

Benno looked up with his mouth agape and held his hands up. "Are you out of your frickin' mind, Lloyd? You shot a guy and we kidnapped two innocent people, one of whom, in case you didn't know, is a rabbi! You know what that means, don't you? We're going to have the FBI on our ass. If you think things were shitty in Wasatch, well that's going to seem like a low security house compared to where they're goin' to throw our asses. Providing the guard don't die. If he dies it's a sharp needle and cold juice for us."

"Benno, it just means we have to improvise, my friend. Instead of drivin' to Wyoming, we're goin' to walk."

Benno leaned forward. "Walk? What the hell do you mean, walk?"

"It means we'll have to change our plans, that's what it means. We'll ditch this old Jeep and strike out on foot for the Wyoming border and the good life. And I've decided we'll take the broad and the preacher man with us. You know what they say, Benno, in for a penny, in for a pound. Now just sit back and let me think."

CHAPTER 13

When Roberto left the police station, he returned to the pharmacy to pick up Clyde's meds. He thought he'd return home, but after sitting in his truck and thinking for a few minutes, he decided to give Jesse Martinson a call and see if she wanted to get a cup of coffee. She'd told him she enjoyed it when they had a cup of coffee after her first day in the hat box and hoped they could do it again sometime. He retrieved the slip of paper with her phone number from his wallet and re-entered the pharmacy, wondering if they would let him use their phone. Roberto just didn't think there was any sense in owning a cell phone. The pharmacist, who felt he owed Roberto a favor, gladly consented to his request.

She answered on the second ring and sounded somewhat surprised and excited to hear from him. She agreed to meet him at the coffee shop close to the outpatient clinic.

En route, Roberto wondered what had possessed him to call her. He must be at least thirty years older than she was. He shrugged. "What the hell, she suggested it."

Roberto loved the Good Cup coffee shop. It was the perfect tranquil retreat after a long session in the hat box. The aroma of freshly brewed, strong Colombian coffee mixed with newly baked pastries stimulated his salivary glands and allowed his clouded mind to clear. With the first sip of steaming hot coffee, always ordered black, he could feel mental trauma and physical tension induced by the session begin to ease.

When he entered the quaint confines of the Good Cup, Julia, his favorite waitress, smiled as she waved and pointed to an empty booth in the back. She held up an empty cup. He returned the smile. "Make it two. I'm waiting for a friend."

He had just reached the booth when Jesse Martinson entered and immediately began looking for him. He stood and waved, somewhat sheepishly, to get her attention. She looked more relaxed than the first day he met her. And that made her more attractive, not startlingly beautiful, but nice to look at. She wore her dishwater-blonde hair short which made her appear taller than her estimated five foot eight. And he liked how the end of her nose turned up just a bit. She had three small chocolate-colored moles on her right cheek that formed an almost perfect triangle with the smallest and lightest colored at the acme. But it was her steel-blue eyes that got him. He felt like they reached out and froze him in place. He couldn't look away if he wanted to.

"Thanks for coming. If I remember correctly, you like strong coffee so I took it upon myself to order a cup for you."

"Thanks for inviting me. I must say that I was more than a little surprised to hear from you. And, yes, I do like strong coffee. I'm impressed that you remembered. So, what prompted the invite, if I may ask?"

"I was in the neighborhood and the thought popped into my head. Don't ask me why. So I figured what the heck."

"What brought you to this neighborhood?"

"My neighbor, old fellow named Clyde, either can't or won't drive, so whenever I'm in town I pick up his meds for him."

"That's very neighborly of you, Rob." She took a sip of her steaming coffee before continuing. "I got a hint of who you are in our session, but I think I'd like to know more about you. If you don't mind, that is."

He tasted his coffee and paused a moment before beginning. "Not much to tell, really. Growing up I always dreamed of becoming a member of the Special Forces. I loved their motto: *De Oppresso Liber*. Liberate the Oppressed.

Damn, I still think it's cool. Well, anyway, I was sent to 'Nam, and during my second tour I was leading an assault force to rescue some trapped brass. But my squad was wiped out, except for my medic and me. That was a helluva an ordeal. They sent me home, but I couldn't hold a job and I drank a lot. I didn't know what was happening to me until I was diagnosed as having PTSD. So, eventually I thought I needed a geographic fix and relocated out here." He took another sip of coffee and added, "I guess I've found my little niche in life."

"What about a family?"

Pointing at himself he said, "Who, me? No, I'm afraid not." He stared at his coffee cup and began turning it in circles before returning his gaze to Jesse. "Who'd want an old, broken down, war-scarred vet like me anyway? But, hey. What about you? What's your story?"

She hesitated a moment before answering and looked at this man who somehow in a short time was triggering emotions she wasn't sure had existed. She guessed him at six-two and a buck ninety-five, and he had the darkest blue, but clear, eyes. And his jaw was square and looked so solid . . . It was somehow sexy. Or was it his hair, which she noted he wore Mark Harmon, *NCIS*-style with hints of gray at the temples. She realized she was staring and coughed to regain the moment. "Who, me? I'm afraid I'm pretty boring. I'm kind of like you in that I also dreamed of the military as a child. After the Storm I needed a job, and with my parents both in law enforcement, it seemed natural to follow in their footsteps. But I had this PTSD to deal with and, hopefully, TJ can screw my hat on correctly or tight or whatever it is you guys say about him."

"Family?"

"No." She pointed at her head. "Not until it's all straight up here."

Roberto pushed back in the booth and glanced at his watch. "It's getting late, Jess. I think I'd better get going. But, hey, thanks for taking the time to visit." He pushed his coffee cup to the side before adding, "I've, ah, I've really enjoyed this, and, ah, I'd like to do it again some time. I guess you can tell I'm a bit out of practice at this type of stuff."

She smiled and said, "I'd like that, too, Rob."

"Then how about coming out to my place tomorrow night for dinner? You know, no strings attached. Just two friends enjoying some good food and some companionship."

"I'd like that, Rob. But on one condition. I bring the dessert."

They shook hands and Rob gave her the directions to his home. On the way to his truck he thought that it went surprisingly well. But now he'd better make a trip to the market and get something for their dinner. And he'd better pick up some wine. He'd have to ask John at the off-sale what kind of wine ladies liked because he didn't have a clue and he wasn't sure if it was proper etiquette to offer a lady a can of beer. He checked his watch again and decided he'd bring Clyde his meds in the morning. He hoped he'd be okay until then.

CHAPTER 14

Lloyd saw the small trail leading off 212 to the right, but it looked like it had been used too often to be safe. About a mile farther he noted another barely perceptible trail, slowed enough to make the turn, and headed into the foothills. This driveway was actually no more than two ruts with grass between them, lined by mature hardwoods interspersed with majestic pines providing a canopy-like effect. He glanced over his shoulder. "This looks perfect. Hold on cuz it's goin' to be a little rough."

Benno looked at the still-trembling lady and motioned with both palms down. "Cool it," he whispered. "Everything's going to be okay."

She rolled her eyes and dabbed at the tears tinged with mascara, streaming down her face like two small black rivers. She tossed her head back and appeared, at least momentarily, to regain some composure. "Yeah, right," she whispered. "You guys are nuts, and you know you won't get away with this."

Benno, with as much machismo as he could conjure, stared at her for a moment. His shoulders sagged, and he shook his head. "It wasn't supposed to happen this way," He whispered. He nodded at Lloyd. "I don't know what got into him. He's nuts and I'm just as afraid as you are."

She leaned toward Benno and patted his knee "Please let me and the rabbi go," she whispered. "We'll just be a burden." She nodded at Lloyd. "Please don't let him hurt us."

Benno nodded. "Don't worry none. I won't."

Lloyd, holding tightly onto the steering wheel as the Jeep's suspension was repeatedly tested, gave them a fleeting look over his shoulder. "What the hell is going on back there? Don't talk to that bitch. You just stay focused. Hear me? And keep that gun up, just in case. Got it? I think I see a house up ahead. Hopefully we can get some supplies there before we head out."

CHAPTER 15

Clyde was napping in his rocking chair when he heard the vehicle approach. It might be Roberto with his medications. He would need one of the Coreg tablets tonight and the Lasix first thing in the morning. His knees creaked in protest as he slowly stood. He laid the Bible he had been reading before falling asleep on the chair and limped to the window. He pulled the curtain back, providing him a glimpse of a black Jeep. *Now who might that be?*

Britches, his aging black lab, began to stir from her favorite spot in front of the fireplace. Her nose in the air, she ambled toward Clyde with a low growl beginning to emanate from the back of her throat.

Clyde, his eyes riveted on the Jeep, reached down and stroked his favorite girl's head. "Now you just be quiet there, Young Lady. And try to be hospitable for a change." But Clyde was already becoming a bit anxious as he got his first glimpse of the man exiting the Jeep. The unexpected visitor, who looked quite unkempt, pointed and shook a finger. *He must have someone with him.* The trespasser approached the entrance to Clyde's home.

Clyde leaned down and stroked Britches' head again, saying, more to reassure himself than his friend, "It's going to be okay, Girl. Now you just behave, okay?"

Clyde opened the door just as Lloyd was about to knock. "What can I do for you, young man? Are you lost?"

The young man glanced toward the Jeep. "Yeah, I guess I turned off on the wrong road. My friend is sick and I was wondering if I might use your phone to call a doctor."

"Well, I don't have no phone. Never knew a reason to get one, I guess. And I never needed one either."

"Really? Well, do you think I might at least get a glass of water for him?"

"Sure enough. You wait right here and I'll get you one." Clyde turned to walk back into the safety of his home, but before he could close the door, the intruder pushed him into the house.

Clyde stumbled and Britches bared her teeth and began to growl. The invader took one step into the house and kicked the still-growling dog in the chest and then in the head. Clyde, who had regained his balance, turned toward his assailant with a feeling of bewilderment that rapidly changed to one of anger and then sadness. He limped to Britches' side and tried to comfort her by stroking her back. "I don't know what you want, Mister, but I'll tell you that I don't have anything you'd want. And you didn't need to hurt my dog. She didn't do anything to you."

The intruder pulled the .38 handgun from his pocket and knelt on one knee. Pointing it first at Clyde and then at Britches, he stared at Clyde. "Now you listen to me, Old Man. I do need some things and I do believe you have what I want. You just do as I say, and you and your mangy old hound won't get hurt. You don't how lucky you are that you don't have no phone. Now I'm going to get my partner and you just stay right where you're at. Understand?"

As the man stood up, Clyde glimpsed the ugliest tattoo he'd ever seen. He wondered who in their right mind would put a spider on their neck. The invader walked to the door and whistled. "Benno, get your ass in here and bring the other two with you! Now!" Turning to Clyde, he said, "Okay, Old Man, I'm goin' to need any guns you may have, some food, warm coats, and blankets. You wouldn't happen to have a four-wheeler in that small shed outside, would ya?"

Clyde just stared at this contemptible excuse for a man who had invaded his privacy and injured his dog. When he didn't reply, the man squatted down and held the pistol to the back of Britches' head. "Old Timer, I'd suggest you don't screw with me. Now I asked you a question. I'm goin' to give you just five seconds to answer and if you don't, well it's bye-bye Poochie." He held up one finger at a time.

When he reached four Clyde spoke up. "Okay, I'll give you whatever I have that you want. Just don't hurt my dog anymore."

"Right answer, Old Man. Now, once again, do you have a four-wheeler in that shed outside?"

"Yeah, I've got one. It's an old one, but it still runs pretty well." He sighed. "And it's full of gas."

The door opened and a lady entered his house followed by a man in a black suit, white shirt, and black tie, wearing a black hat. His beard was a heavy five o'clock shadow. He was followed by a second man Clyde assumed to be his assailant's partner, the one called Benno. Another obvious reprobate, but this one looked quite anxious and seemed to be shrouded in a false bravado.

The lady knelt down and began petting Britches. "You cruel, ignominious son of a bitch. So this is how you manifest your supposed manhood, huh? You shoot an unarmed guard, steal because you can't get or hold a job, kidnap a lady and a rabbi, slap the lady, push around an elderly gentleman, and hurt a dog." She clapped in a slow, mocking way. "So what do you do for an encore, Mister Macho? Screw a sheep?" She continued clapping and began to laugh. In a few seconds, her laughter turned to hysterical shrieking.

The man in the suit, who looked like a rabbi, approached his fellow prisoner, but Spider Tattoo pushed him against the door and backhanded the laughing lady across the face. The crack of bone against flesh resounded through the small, enclosed space. Stumbling backward, she caught herself on the rocking chair Clyde had been sitting in when his world was turned upside down. She stopped shrieking hysterically, but the intruder pressed the pistol between her eyebrows.

"Lloyd, for God's sake back off! Leave her alone!" Benno yelled.

Lloyd wheeled and stared at him. The right side of his neck began to twitch, so his tarantula appearing to be crawling up his neck. He pointed the handgun at Benno, "So what's the deal with you, Benno. Got somethin' for the lady, have ya?"

Benno raised his arms. "Jeez, Lloyd, you know that ain't the thing. I just don't want to hurt nobody. That was our deal, remember? No one gets hurt. Just get the easy cash and head for Wyoming and the good life."

Lloyd turned again to the lady, who was now kneeling on the floor and clasping both hands to her mouth in an attempt to stifle a scream. "You say one more thing like that and I will shoot you, Bitch. Got it? Now get up, get your ass over here, and help us get the things we need. We're gettin' out of here today."

Lloyd looked at Clyde, who was still holding Britches, who was moaning. "Where's your guns and ammo, Old Man? And we're goin' to need some coats and blankets." Pointing at the kitchen with the handgun, he looked at Benno. "You look in the kitchen for any food we can take with us. Have the broad help you. The old man's got a four-wheeler we'll take to haul all the shit we need. You can get that outta the shed when you have the food together."

Lloyd took a pack of Marlboros from his shirt pocket, and with one flick he opened his Bic lighter and had a flame shooting from it. He lit the cigarette, inhaled deeply, and blew the smoke toward Clyde, who was gesturing toward a small closet next to the kitchen. "Guns and bullets are in there. I have one rifle and one pistol. That's all."

Lloyd took another deep drag on the cigarette and pointed it at Clyde. "I suppose you're one of them assholes that don't like nobody smokin' in your house. Shame on me. I guess I shoulda asked first." He snickered as he took the cigarette from his mouth and flicked it onto the small rug in front of Clyde's sink. While staring at Clyde, he ground the cigarette into the rug with his toe. "Sorry about that." He opened the closet door and retrieved a .308 with a variable 3x9 Leupold scope as well as a .44 magnum pistol. He pointed the .38 Ruger at the rabbi. "Preacher Man. Get over here and hold this stuff."

The rabbi folded his arms across his chest and shrugged. "I shall have no part of handling any weapons."

"You either hold and carry these weapons or you will feel their sting. Now what's it gonna be? And I'd rather not waste any ammo on you. Now move it!"

The rabbi slowly dropped his arms and stared defiantly at Lloyd before moving toward the closet. Lloyd held out the rifle. "Hold this." He glanced at Benno. "How you doin' with the grub?" Before Benno could respond, Lloyd turned his attention to his female captive. "You go into the bedroom and grab a pillowcase and bring it here so I have somethin' to put the ammo in." He picked up the Ruger .44 magnum pistol and turned it around in his hand, appearing to admire its beauty, before handing it to the rabbi.

His female hostage returned from the bedroom and threw a pillowcase on the floor just out of Lloyd's reach. She walked into the kitchen, where she handed a second one to Benno. "I thought you could use this for the food."

It took Lloyd and Benno about fifteen minutes to pile the food, blankets, a sleeping bag, the weapons and ammo, and three jackets on the kitchen table. Lloyd nodded at Benno. "You go out and get the four-wheeler started and bring it up to the house. We'll tie this shit up somehow and be ready to get outta here in about another five minutes. I want to be in the woods before dark."

"Lloyd, my main man, don't you think it would be smarter to stay here the night where it's warm and dry and then leave at first light tomorrow? I, ah, I think it would be the smart move." Benno smiled. "But you're the boss."

"Damn right. I'm the boss and I'm in charge, and don't you forget it. And like I said, we're leavin' tonight. Now get your ass movin' and do as I tell you." He pointed his .38 at Benno. "Now go get that four-wheeler. Now!"

"Jeez, Lloyd, I thought we were partners and made decisions together."

"Well, that all changed back at the jewelry store." He looked at Clyde, who was still sitting on the floor holding Britches. "Got any duct tape around this dump, Old Man?"

Clyde didn't respond immediately, so Lloyd walked over and kicked him in the leg, "Answer me or, as I told you before, I'll shoot your pooch."

"You are one despicable human being. You know that, don't you?" Pausing as if to let his words sink in, he nodded toward the kitchen. "There's a roll of duct tape in the top drawer on the right side of the sink. Now please take all these things you're set on stealing and leave me and my dog alone."

Lloyd lashed out and kicked Clyde again in the leg before turning toward the kitchen. He found the duct tape in the drawer as well as two flashlights. He used the tape to begin securing the blankets and sleeping bag. At the sound of the four-wheeler, he looked at his two captives. "Take this shit out to Benno and tell him to get it on the four-wheeler. I'll be out in a coupla minutes and then we're headin' out. Also tell Benno to grab the atlas outta the Jeep. Now get goin'. Oh and, Lady, before you go I'd suggest you get ridda those shoes and put the old man's shoes on." He pointed at her feet. "Those ain't goin' to do you any good where we're goin'."

She stared at him with mouth agape.

"There's a pair of my wife's old boots in the same closet where you got the guns," Clyde said. "They ought to fit you okay. Go ahead and take 'em. He's right, you will need something different out there. There's also an old warm coat of hers in there. Take that as well. They aren't doing me any good anymore."

She smiled warmly at Clyde. "Thank you very kindly. I do appreciate your kindness." She gave Lloyd a mock salute. "Anything else… Boss?"

"Just get the boots and coat and get your ass outta here!"

She sauntered to the closet where she retrieved a pair of Sorel boots and a worn but intact light gold, down-filled coat that had a dull red stocking cap and gloves stuffed in the pockets. She looked at Clyde and smiled warmly as she took off her thin jacket and put on his wife's coat. She took even longer taking off her shoes, putting on the Sorels, and slowly tying the laces. As she was putting on the second boot, she looked up at Lloyd, shook her head, and snickered.

"What the hell's so goddamn funny? I told you to get the lead out." He kicked Clyde again in the leg. "Now, if you don't get your ass movin' I'm going to cause him some real pain and it'll be your fault."

She rose, straightened the coat, put the gloves on and stared at Lloyd for a second. "You are one poor, miserable piece of shit, waste of good oxygen." She looked at Clyde with sorrowful, tear-filled eyes. "I'm so sorry for what these men…" She nodded toward Lloyd. "Especially this piece of shit, have done to you. I'll say some prayers for you. Goodbye, Sir." And with that she exited through the door.

Lloyd looked down at Clyde. "It's a good thing somebody feels sorry for you because I sure as hell don't." Lloyd grabbed one of the old wooden, slat-backed kitchen chairs and pushed it toward Clyde, who held onto Britches just a bit tighter. "How about you get your sorry ass up into this here chair."

"Why? Why don't you just leave and let me and Britches be."

"Because I want you up here where I can make sure you ain't goin' to call anybody for help."

"How am I going to do that when I told you earlier that I don't have a phone?"

"Just get your sorry ass up here. Now!"

Clyde deliberately took his time pulling himself to a standing position and limped to the chair. Lloyd wrapped the duct tape tightly around his chest and arms and then around his legs, hitting the injured leg again. "Well now, Old Man, that should hold you until someone finds you." Chuckling, he added, "At least when you die you won't mess up the floor."

"What about my dog?"

"It's your lucky day, Old Man. I've decided not to kill the mutt." Lloyd left the house, leaving Clyde to wonder if Roberto would find him and Britches in time.

CHAPTER 16

The night sky erupted—again. Roberto recognized the AK-47s firing at them from all directions—*slap, slap, slap.* The darting lights accompanying the staccato fire of the Viet Cong weapons of death were followed by the sharp cracking of tree limbs breaking, the dull thuds emitted from human flesh, and the occasional cry of a young man about to give his life for his country, "Medic! Medic! Oh please, God, I'm hit! Sarge! Please help me! Mediccccccc!"

The unceasing rifle fire was followed by the unrelenting, deafening explosions of the mortars and grenades, all seemingly aimed specifically at an acne-faced, scared-shitless GI. It left a few soldiers writhing in the agony of their life-ending wounds and too many lying in the stillness of death.

As quickly as it began, the attack was over. Roberto surveyed the carnage, realizing the only two survivors were himself and the medic who was rocking back and forth while cradling the bandaged dead body of yet another teenager. Roberto slowly made his way to the medic, who was sobbing uncontrollably. He looked up at his sergeant and said through the gut-wrenching, chest-heaving sobs, "I'm so sorry, Sarge. I'm so, so sorry. I failed again."

Before he could attempt to comfort his medic, Roberto heard another mortar round coming toward them. He dove to the ground and covered the medic, who refused to let go of the body he felt he had failed to save. The round exploded about twenty-five yards to their left, scattering debris over the three of them.

Roberto awakened again, drenched in perspiration, throwing the blankets and pillow off the bed and yelling.

"STOP FOR GOD'S SAKE! STOP! THAT'S ENOUGH! GOD DAMN ENOUGH!"

He threw his legs over the side of the bed and began rubbing at his neck while trying to wipe some of the perspiration from his face with the remaining bed sheet. When his breathing and heart rate had slowed, he made his way to the kitchen, where the ice water awaited him. Again he wondered when and if the nightmares would ever end.

Roberto's gut told him the recuperation times were increasing. However, his mind suggested that he never wholly recovered from one nightmare to the next. This time he guessed he stood at the sink about ten minutes, pouring one pitcher of ice water after another over the back of his head and neck before the tension gradually eased. He felt too fatigued to go on his usual morning run. Besides, he had to take Clyde's medications to him.

He toweled his head, opened the door, and called for Bogey. "You're on your own this morning, Pal." His canine partner sat with his head lolled to one side and looked up at his master with his large, sad, brown eyes. Roberto leaned down and scratched his ears, then pointed outside. "Go on, do your thing. I'll take a shower and then let you back in. Now go." With that his large, slobbering companion bolted out the door.

Roberto glanced at the clock on the mantel over his fireplace. He had about five minutes for a steaming hot shower to loosen up his taut muscles before heading over to Clyde's. After that he would need to return and clean up his house before beginning to prepare for the dinner with Jesse Martinson tonight. He shook his head as he turned on the shower, still wondering how he'd let his guard down enough to invite a woman to his home, to say nothing of making dinner for her. *Must be getting old and soft.*

When he had finished showering and dressing, he opened the door for Bogey, making a mental note to clean his bathroom as well. He couldn't remember the last time a woman had used his bathroom. Did he need anything he didn't have? Well, it would just have to do this time.

While Bogey crunched the large pellets of dog food his master had put into his dish, Roberto put the bag containing Clyde's medications into the canvas bag he usually secured to the back of his four-wheeler. He smiled at Bogey. "You about finished there, Old Boy? We've got to get going. Big day ahead of us you know."

Bogey looked up at his master and evidently understood because he quit eating and walked to the open door. Roberto locked the door, and the two headed for the storage shed, at the edge of his property, where the four-wheeler awaited. He knew Bogey enjoyed these one-mile trips through the woods to Clyde's home. It gave him a chance for some good exercise.

Roberto left the trail and entered the northeast edge of the clearing where Clyde's modest three-room log cabin stood. He immediately became aware of two things: there was no smoke coming from the chimney, and there was an old black Jeep in front of the door. He eased up to the unrecognized vehicle and hopped off his four-wheeler. He took a quick look inside, but did not see anything that would identify the owner. Roberto began to feel the short hairs on the back of his neck become stiff, just like when his platoon was on patrol and there were gooks close by. Instinctively, he reached to the small of his back and silently cursed himself for forgetting his handgun.

He dropped into a crouch and hurried to the small kitchen window on the north side of Clyde's home. Easing up along the wall, he pressed his ear as close to the window as he could get and thought he could hear a dog moaning. Taking a chance, he looked through the window and saw Clyde taped to a chair and slumped forward.

He ran around to the door and threw it open, remembering that Clyde never locked it despite the numerous warnings Roberto had given him. He dropped to his knees and carefully probed Clyde's neck to feel for a pulse. Roberto began tearing at the tape while talking to his neighbor, friend and confidant, but there was no response. When the duct tape had been torn, freeing the elderly, frail man, he carried Clyde to his bed. He seemed very cold, and his breathing was raspy. Roberto grabbed the extra blanket Clyde always kept at the foot of his bed and gently covered him. He ran into the kitchen, but then remembered Clyde didn't own a phone. He had told Roberto on numerous occasions, "Never had a need for one, Son. Not with you so close and willing to come by once in a while."

"Yeah, well, now would be a damn good time to have one, Old Man," he said aloud. He ran his fingers through his hair. *And no cell phone. Dammit. I guess I'd better break down and get one. Well, only one thing to do.* "Bogey, guard." He knew with that simple command he could leave Clyde here safely while he rode his four-wheeler home and called an ambulance and the police. He bolted through the still-open door, climbed on his four-wheeler, and began the one-mile ride home, constantly reminding himself that he needed to arrive safely if he was going to help Clyde.

CHAPTER 17

When Roberto exited the woods, he was met with yet another surprise. There was a Jeep Wrangler in front of his home. He hit the brakes on his four-wheeler and turned the handlebars, causing it to slide sideways before coming to a stop. *Who's here and what's with all the Jeeps today?* Jesse Martinson exited her vehicle with a soft warm smile that immediately vanished when she noted the look on Roberto's face. He sprinted toward his door calling over his shoulder, "What the hell are you doing here already?"

He entered the house and left her standing in the yard with her eyes wide and mouth open. She raised her arms with palms skyward. "Hello and it's good to see you too!"

Roberto poked his head out the door and Jesse noticed that he had a phone tucked between his left ear and shoulder. He waved to her to come in. She leaned into her Wrangler, lifted out a box, and began walking to the house. He was still talking on the phone when she extended her gift-bearing arms and mouthed, "I brought dessert."

"Thanks and hurry. I'll meet you at the start of his driveway so you'll be sure to find it." There was a pause, and he added, "Thanks."

He took a deep breath and smiled apologetically. "Sorry about that. How about if we start over. Hello, Jesse. I'm surprised to see you here so early."

"Well, I thought I'd come early and see what your place looks like in the daylight and, perhaps, take a walk in the woods before dinner." She pointed toward the phone. "So what's going on?"

"It's kind of a long story, but the short of the long, which I can give you later, is that I picked up some medications yesterday for my neighbor, Clyde Ashburn, who's an eighty-two-year-old widower who lives about a mile from here." He nodded in the direction of his neighbor's home. "When I got there this morning, I found an abandoned Jeep in his yard and Clyde duct taped to a chair and unresponsive. You gotta understand that he's got a lot of heart problems. So I put him on his bed, covered him up, and left Bogey to guard him and his place so I could return here and call an ambulance. Before you ask, I'll tell you—Clyde doesn't have a phone. Said he's never needed one, until today that is. His road is essentially unused so I'll have to go out there so they can find it." He pointed toward the highway.

"How about you put this dessert in your refrigerator while I grab a different jacket and change from shoes to boots, and I'll come with you."

"I have to warn you that this isn't going to be any easy ride."

"Don't worry about me. You'll soon learn that I can handle myself." By the time Roberto got to his four-wheeler, Jesse was already on the back. She smiled. "Let's go, Captain."

He turned the key to start the Polaris 500 EFI and shifted into high gear. "Hold on tight!" Despite a firm grip on the passenger handles, Jesse was thrown back when Roberto squeezed the throttle. The ride was anything but smooth as the 728-pound machine went airborne more than once. When they reached the highway, Roberto slowed just enough to make a safe sliding turn to the right before squeezing the throttle tight again. He left the four-wheeler running in Clyde's driveway and hopped off to make it easier for Jesse to disembark. He helped her off the machine, placed both hands on her shoulders, and looked into her eyes. "How about if you stay here so the ambulance knows where to turn? I want to go up to Clyde's and check on him." He placed his right hand on her cheek. "Please. I'd just feel better."

Jesse could sense her new friend's concern for his elderly neighbor. She smiled and touched his left cheek. "Sure. I'll be okay and I'll ride up with them. They should be here soon."

She was mildly shocked when he leaned in and gave her a quick kiss on her cheek. "Thanks.

"And here, just in case." He reached down near the small of his back and handed her a .40-caliber Glock 23 handgun. "Be careful. It's loaded. I'll see you in a bit."

Jesse stood holding the handgun as Roberto literally jumped onto the purring ATV, squeezed the throttle, and roared off. She touched her left cheek where he had kissed her. She could still feel his lips, and this made her smile. This was a feeling she could not remember having in years.

Her military instincts told her to check the pistol. It had a 13-round clip loaded with .40 caliber S&W cartridges, and there was one in the chamber. She'd been taught that this was the ideal cartridge for personal defense. She liked Roberto even more.

ROBERTO SLID THE POLARIS TO A STOP just in front of Clyde's main entry. He ran into the house and to the bedroom. Clyde was still breathing, thank God, but he appeared to be having more difficulty than before Roberto left. He placed his index finger on his unresponsive friend's carotid artery. His pulse was faster and weaker than before. Roberto grabbed the other pillow and put it under Clyde's head. He had to do something and maybe it would help a little bit.

He returned to the kitchen to retrieve a cool washcloth to wipe Clyde's brow and heard Britches moaning. Roberto looked into the small living room. Britches' tail was slowly wagging. Bogey was lying close to her with his head on the floor, staring at her as if to will her to get up and play with him. Roberto ran over to the two canines, knelt down, and scratched Bogey's ears. With his other hand he gently stroked Britches' back and chest. She was breathing easily and responded to his touch with increased movement of her tail. He looked at his best friend. "Good job, Bogey. Don't worry, she'll be okay." He pointed at Bogey. "Stay."

By the time he reached Clyde's bedside, he could hear the ambulance on the highway. He began wiping Clyde's brow with the washcloth. "You hang in there, Old Man," he said quietly. "They'll be here any minute and they're going to help you."

IN LESS THAN FIVE MINUTES THE EMTS were in the house tending to Clyde, who was still unresponsive. Jesse was at Roberto's side. She put her arm around him and began massaging his upper back. "He's going to be okay, Roberto," she whispered.

He gave her what she thought was the warmest and kindest smile she had ever seen. He put his arm around her and squeezed her tightly to his side. The EMTs had an IV line in. They checked Clyde's vital signs and turned his oxygen on. The obvious lead EMT approached Roberto while her two associates continued to administer care. "You happen to know anything about this man's medical history? Any medications he takes or anything else that will help us?"

"The only thing I know is that he asked me to pick up a couple of prescriptions for him yesterday." He pointed to the kitchen. "I put them on the counter next to the sink when I came in earlier and found him on the floor. I have no idea what they are or what else he takes."

The lead EMT began walking to the kitchen. "Would you mind checking the medicine cabinet in his bathroom for me to see if there are any other pill bottles there?" She picked up the pharmacy bag and retrieved the bottles. "You guys about ready to go?" she asked the other two EMTs. The young, bearded emergency medical tech nodded. "Jake, you go call it in and turn the bus around," the lead EMT said. "I want to be moving in three minutes."

While she was looking at the two prescription bottles and writing the information in her notebook, Roberto returned from the bedroom and handed her three more bottles. He looked at her nametag. "Excuse me, Ms. Bert, but can you tell me if he's going to be okay?"

She glanced up. "It's Bert." She pointed at her name tag. "We just go by first names. Your friend's vitals are stable. He's going to need some work, but I think he'll make it. I know the doc whose name is on these prescription bottles, and he's a good one. Now if you'll excuse me, we'll finish our work and get him out of here. We'll take him to the Good Shepherd Hospital in Billings." With that she looked past Roberto. "You ready, Sue?"

When her associate nodded, she tucked her notebook into her backpack and assisted with transferring Clyde to a gurney. Roberto held the door open and patted his elderly friend on the arm as he was taken to the waiting ambulance. With Jesse holding his arm, Roberto said, "Don't you worry, Old Buddy. You're going to be just fine, and I promise you I will get the sons-a-bitches that did this to you." Jesse noticed that there were tears streaming down Roberto's cheeks and that he was doing his best to stifle an imminent sob.

CHAPTER 18

Lloyd sat on a stump smoking yet another cigarette close to the small campfire. Unblinking, he absently kicked at the tuft of grass. He picked up a small stone and tossed it in the direction of his captives. *I need a few minutes just to do some figurin' without havin' to think of those assholes.*

He estimated they had traveled about five miles the first day before stopping to make camp last night. He also figured they could have traveled a lot farther if it hadn't been for the rabbi. The preacher man obviously wasn't the outdoors type, and he was in piss-poor physical condition. Lloyd also knew it probably didn't help that he rode the four-wheeler and made the other three walk. But he figured what the hell, he was the leader of this group, and he deserved some privileges. He knew the travel was going to be tough and kind of hoped that Benno would make it, but if he didn't, tough shit. And he didn't really give a rat's ass about the lady and the rabbi.

He had allowed Benno to make the small campfire this morning so they could at least have some coffee. It would be better than drinking that stream water they drank last night to wash down the beef jerky they'd found at the old man's house. The lady was sitting with her back to a white pine tree and rubbing her feet before putting her boots back on. He tossed a small stone in her direction to get her attention. "I know…" He nodded at the rabbi. "That he's a preacher man, but I don't know nothin' about you. What's your name?"

She looked at him incredulously, shook her head, and resumed rubbing her feet. Lloyd walked over and looked down at her. "Look, Lady. You can do this the easy way, or we'll just have to do it the hard way. Now, once again, what the hell's your name?"

She narrowed her eyes. "You do know, don't you, that you are a despicable, repulsive, sick human being? You know that, right? So why should I tell you my name?" She stared at him and spit on the ground close to his shoes.

Lloyd took one step and kicked her in the left shin. She grabbed her leg and rolled onto her side. "Why'd you do that, you creep?"

"Because I told you I want to know your name. Now, are you going to tell me or are we going to play some more games?"

"It's Sheila. Sheila Westburg." Tears streamed down her cheeks. "Satisfied?"

Lloyd threw his cigarette butt at her chest. It landed next to her and he ground the butt into the moist soil, making sure his foot touched her. He walked back to their campfire. He squatted down, grabbed the coffee pot, and poured himself another cup of coffee. "I want to be ready to leave here in about five minutes." He looked directly at his compatriot. "Benno, bring me that atlas. And grab me another pack of butts from the four-wheeler."

Benno picked up the atlas and pack of cigarettes and walked over to the campfire. "Why'd you kick the lady, Lloyd? She didn't do nothin' wrong."

Lloyd grabbed the atlas and stuffed the cigarettes into his shirt pocket. He stared maliciously at Benno for a second before raising his hand like he was about to strike his former cellmate. "What's the matter with you, you spineless little piece of shit? You goin' soft on me, huh? Got somethin' for the broad, do ya?" He threw the atlas on the ground and pulled out Clyde's Ruger Redhawk .44 magnum handgun that he had tucked between his belt and jeans. He cocked the hammer and pushed the muzzle into Benno's forehead. "I oughta just blow you away right now and make my life and this job a helluva lot easier!" He pressed the Redhawk so hard into Benno's forehead it caused Benno to stumble back a couple of steps.

Benno's mouth dropped open and he raised his hands. "Jeez, Lloyd, I ain't soft on the broad!" He seemed to be trying to force a smile. "You know it's just you and me, Partner." He gestured at the rabbi. "These two, and especially the broad, don't mean nothin' to me. Hell, shoot the both of 'em right now. I don't care!"

Lloyd dropped the Ruger and wiped his brow with the back of his dirt-stained sleeve, leaving a mud smear on his forehead. "Oh close your trap, you dipshit, before you piss your pants. Put out the fire and get the stuff loaded on the four-wheeler so we can get outta here. Never know when they'll start comin' after us."

He glanced at the rabbi, who was helping Sheila to her feet. "Let's get goin'. And you two better not hold us up, or I'll leave your dead carcasses for the bears." Lloyd tucked the handgun between his belt and jeans and walked toward the Polaris Sportsman 300. He figured they needed to make thirty to forty miles today.

CHAPTER 19

Jake heard the siren and had to wait for the Carbon County Sheriff's vehicle, trailed by an unmarked Crown Vic, to enter the clearing in front of Clyde's house before he could depart with his still unresponsive patient. A deputy exited the sheriff's car but left the LED-based light bar flashing. Roberto thought he recognized the man getting out of the dust-covered, nondescript black Crown Vic as the same detective he had spoken to after the pharmacy incident.

The deputy walked up to Roberto, who stood at Clyde's door with his arm still around Jesse. His tears had dried like a dry creek bed after a late summer rain.

"Good morning. I'm Deputy Matt Thornton from the Carbon County Sheriff's Department in Red Lodge. Am I correct in assuming that you are Mr. Roberto DeLaCroix and that you placed the 911 call?"

Roberto dropped his arm from Jesse's waist, "Yes, Sir. I'm DeLaCroix and I placed the call." He looked past the young deputy. "Detective Lindsberg, I believe. We meet again so soon." He put his arm around Jesse's shoulders and gave her a slight squeeze. "Gentlemen, this is my friend Jesse Martinson. Now, how can I help you?"

Thornton nodded toward the detective. "Because of the possibility this attack could be linked to a crime committed in Billings yesterday, where two perpetrators robbed an armored car, shot their guard, and kidnapped two people, I took the liberty of calling the Billings PD and asked if they would like to become involved right from the get go. Detective Lindsberg, who I understand you have met previously, had fortuitously been assigned to investigate that crime and agreed to come with me."

The detective walked up to Roberto, grinned slightly, and extended his right hand. "Mr. DeLaCroix. Good to see you again, but I must say that lately you've led a very active life, so to speak."

"It would seem."

Deputy Thornton retrieved a small notebook from his left breast pocket. "Perhaps you can tell us what happened."

Roberto nodded toward the door. "How about if we go into Clyde's house and sit down. It'll be a bit more comfortable in there and perhaps…" He turned to Jesse. "My friend here will brew us up a cup of coffee."

Thornton pushed his police issue hat up and rubbed his forehead with the back of his hand. "I'm not sure that's such a good idea. The house, technically, is a crime scene and will need to be gone over by CSI for prints and whatever else they can find. But, on the other hand, a cup of coffee, especially brewed with mountain water, would really hit the spot about now. Ma'am, do you suppose you could ease yourself into the kitchen and brew us up a pot without touching anything else? Or going into any other room?" Jesse smiled and nodded. He looked at Detective Lindsberg. "You think that would be okay?"

"Well, it's pushing protocol a bit, but I suppose we could allow it. However, I do think it would be a good idea, Ms. Martinson, if you wore some gloves."

She nodded, and the detective retrieved a pair of latex gloves from a pocket of his sport coat. Jesse smiled. "Thank you, Sir." She pointed to a picnic table, leaning over with age. "Now if you gentlemen will have a seat at the picnic table over there, I'll see if I can make us some coffee."

CHAPTER 20

Jesse opened the door to Clyde's home and was immediately impressed. It was not what she expected the home of an eighty-two year old man to look like. The house was obviously very clean and orderly, simple, yet elegant. Her eyes were drawn to a clear glass vase with multi-colored wildflowers sitting on a small handmade table. Next to the vase was a picture of an attractive, smiling, gray-haired woman Jesse assumed was Clyde's wife.

The kitchen, just to the right of the table, was small with the centerpiece being a table and two chairs that appeared to also have been handmade. She thought they reflected Clyde's strength, yet they were inviting and looked comfortable. There was a single placemat and plate on the table. The plate, which had a small chip on its edge, had a wildlife scene painted on it depicting a mature buck standing at the edge of a pine forest. Next to the plate was a cup with a matching scene painted on the outside, the inside stained from years of holding strong, hot coffee.

She walked to the sink that was positioned in the middle of the counter and centered under a window adorned with olive-drab curtains and offering an easterly view. Jesse smiled as she drank in the view and thought Clyde and his wife must have loved seeing the sun ease into their lives through this portal every morning while their coffee was brewing on the four-burner stove in the corner. She glanced down at the rug in front of the sink and noted the cigarette butt that had been ground into the rug. This was one more piece of evidence of how intrusive and malicious these people were who had invaded Clyde's home and his life.

She was startled out of her semi-trance when she heard a dog whimpering. She looked up and saw Bogey as he began to stand. She hurried over to him and saw a lab lying on the floor next to a rocking chair. The dog was panting and looking up at her with large, sad brown eyes that attempted to manifest strength while also pleading for help. Jesse patted Bogey's head then knelt beside the obviously injured animal and began to stroke its back. She ran to the door and threw it open. "Rob! Come quick!" Tears began welling in the corners of her eyes. "Clyde's dog is hurt! Hurry!" Then she ran back into the house.

CHAPTER 21

When Jesse entered the house, Roberto led the two investigators to the picnic bench and gestured for the two men to take a seat opposite him. He brushed aside some of nature's gatherings on the table top and folded his hands. "Well, gentlemen, where should we begin?"

Deputy Thornton placed his notebook on the table and nervously began twirling the pen in his fingers. "Mr. DeLaCroix, I—"

But before he could continue, Roberto held up his hand. "Hold it right there, Deputy. It's Roberto, no Mister. Okay?"

"Okay, ah, Roberto?" He looked at Roberto for some signal that he was proceeding correctly and noted his barely perceptible nod. "Ah, I want to begin by telling you that I'm new on the Carbon County force, but I was informed by the sheriff that you've worked with us in the past. Is that correct? You've done a number of search and rescues for us over the years, am I correct?"

"Yes, Sir, that's correct." Rob looked at Detective Lindsberg. "I'm sure the good detective here will tell you that I've also assisted the Billings PD and the Yellowstone County Sheriff's Department with a number of search and rescue operations as well." He grinned. "Can't believe the number of hikers, campers, hunters, and fishermen who just assume because they were Boy Scouts they can wander into the Beartooths without a compass. They sure do eat some humble pie when we find them. So the answer to your question is that yes, I am known and do have a good relationship with the area law enforcement agencies."

Shifting his weight on the bench, the young deputy cleared his throat and scribbled on the notepad. "Good. Could you please, ah, tell me what happened. At least in your own words and to the best of your knowledge. Well, you know the drill."

Roberto smiled. It was always fun working with a rookie. He was about to begin his story when Jesse opened the door and yelled to him about Clyde's dog. He leaped off the bench and raced to the house wondering how he could have possibly forgotten the dogs.

He brushed past Jesse and took the two steps required to be at Bogey's side. From habit he began to scratch his friend's head as he knelt by the whimpering lab. He looked over his shoulder and yelled, "Thornton! Get in here!"

Jesse slid the rocking chair aside so Rob could better attend the injured dog. She saw the still-open Bible. It was open to the book of Ruth. A small photo, matching the one next to the vase, had been used as a bookmark. She picked up the Bible and glanced at the underlined verse. "For wherever you go, I will go; And wherever you lodge, I will lodge; Your people shall be my people, and your God my God. Where you die, I will die, and there will I be buried."

She was still holding the Bible and dabbing at the tears welling up in her eyes, wondering who could possibly hurt a man like Clyde, when Deputy Thornton rushed through the door. "Holy shit, what happened to the dog?"

"I hadn't gotten to that part yet. The guys who beat up old Clyde also did a number on his dog, Britches. She's hurting bad and needs a vet. How about if you and I take her to the vet in Red Lodge?" He nodded at Jesse and Detective Lindsberg. "They can follow and then we can finish up at your office? Work for you, Detective?"

"Yeah, that will work just fine. I'll let my office know and then we'll be right behind you." He looked at Thornton. "I think you need to notify your crime scene investigators so they can get out here and begin their review ASAP. I would suggest you do that before we leave."

Thornton scribbled another hasty note in his notebook while walking to the door. "Whenever you're ready, Roberto, we'll take off."

Roberto had already picked up Britches. "We're right behind you, Deputy." He looked at Jesse. "I'll meet you at the sheriff's office and when we're finished there, we'll go see Clyde." He exited the house with Bogey at his side. "Home, boy." Jesse was looking at him incredulously.

"Don't worry, Jess. Bogey will be just fine until I get back." He shifted the injured dog in his arms and trotted to the waiting deputy's car.

CHAPTER 22

Detective Jonathan Lindsberg and Jesse were waiting at the Carbon County Sheriff's office when Deputy Thornton and Roberto arrived from the veterinarian's clinic. Jesse rushed up to Roberto and threw her arms around his neck. She kissed his cheek and squeezed him hard, catching Roberto off guard. He pulled back slightly, and Jesse looked up at him with a warm smile. "Get used to it, Buddy. Now, how's Britches doing? Will she be all right?"

"Yeah, Dr. Trishman, a lady vet, says the old girl will be just fine. She'll need some IVs and some good old-fashioned TLC for a few days, but then she'll be okay."

Jesse didn't let go of Roberto. "What's going to happen to her with Clyde in the hospital?"

"When the doc says she can go home, I'll take her to my place until Clyde is up and at 'em again. Now how about you let go for a minute so we can finish up with the two patiently waiting gentlemen?"

Jesse dropped her arms but grabbed Roberto's hand and squeezed it. She stood on tiptoes and whispered in his ear. "What's the matter? Embarrassed?" She gave his hand another quick, firm squeeze.

Roberto looked down, hoping time would allow the blush to fade, cleared his throat, and looked at Thornton. "Well, Deputy, where should we meet to finish our discussion?"

Deputy Thornton was blushing as well, thinking his girlfriend would find the same perverse pleasure in embarrassing him. He nodded over his shoulder. "Follow me. We'll use a conference room down the hall."

It took Roberto about fifteen minutes to update the two law enforcement officials about finding the two punks at his home after the convenience store robbery and murder, the incident with the addict at the pharmacy, and finding Clyde at his home.

"If you don't mind my asking, Roberto, how did the young lady here become involved?" Detective Lindsberg gestured toward Jesse. "I mean, only with regard to the investigation, of course."

Jesse put her hand on Roberto's forearm. "If you don't mind, Rob, I'll answer that one."

He grinned and made a sweeping gesture with his arm. "Be my guest, Ms. Martinson." Under his breath he added, "This should be interesting." That earned him a sharp jab in the ribs from Jesse's elbow.

She took a deep breath and began. "Well, it's like this. . ." It only required about three minutes to tell them how she had met Roberto, their subsequent meeting at the coffee shop, his invitation to dinner, and showing up early at his home. "And that's how I came to be involved in this investigation. Gentlemen…" She squeezed Roberto's forearm again. "And, Roberto, this is something I haven't had a chance to even tell you yet. I am a member of the Yellowstone County Sheriff's Department. I have been ever since I got out of the Army. And I have also been involved in some search and rescue operations, although, I will admit, perhaps not to the same extent as my friend here. So, gentlemen, that being said, I would like to be included in this investigation, no matter where it carries us, until we find and bring these assholes to justice."

Roberto shook his head. "Well, jeez, Jess, I don't know—"

Before he could conclude, she raised her hand. "You have nothing to say about this, Mr. DeLaCroix. Remember, you're just someone who happens to be involved because you found your neighbor all busted up and unconscious. You haven't been invited to become involved yet." Her voice rose defiantly. "So don't tell me I can't be a part of this team." She folded her arms across her chest.

The impending stalemate was broken when Detective Lindsberg coughed. "Hold on here just a second. Before you two get into a pissing match that neither wants to be in, let me remind you of something you both know. The decision as to whether either of you or both of you will be involved in any law enforcement operation is not up to you. I suggest I drop you two off at Roberto's place so you can pick up a vehicle. Then you go see Mr. Ashburn at the hospital, and when you're done you come to the Billings PD. I'll go there now, fill in the chief on what we have so far, and when you guys get there, we can discuss things like the adults we're supposed to be. Sound okay to you two?"

When they nodded, he turned to Deputy Thornton. "This will give you some time to present the case to the sheriff and finish your paperwork. After I discuss this with the chief, I'm sure he'll be in touch with the sheriff to discuss how we can coordinate our efforts. Sound about right to you?"

After the deputy nodded, Detective Lindsberg stood. "Well, that's the plan, now let's go work it."

CHAPTER 23

After they'd passed through the revolving entrance doors to the Good Shepherd Hospital, Roberto abruptly stopped, causing Jesse to almost lose her balance. He was standing stiffly with his arms at his sides. His hands were so taut she could see the tendons bulging on the backs of his hands, and the veins on his neck stuck out like blue pencils. For a moment she was afraid they would burst.

"What's the matter, Rob? You look like you've seen a ghost."

"I hate these goddamn places."

Small beads of sweat were forming on his brow, and his unblinking eyes were staring straight ahead. "You know it only takes a few things to start a hospital, don't you, Jess?"

Jesse grabbed his hand and slowly massaged the rough and calloused palm with her thumb. With her other hand, she stroked his whiskered cheek. With a soft, comforting voice, she asked, "What's that, Rob?"

He took a deep breath, glanced around, and grinned. "All you need is an old brick building, an over-waxed tile floor, and antiseptic sprayed by the gallon everywhere. And enough starch to hold an old telegraph pole up in a windstorm." Taking Jesse's hand, he looked deep into her eyes and momentarily thought he was seeing her for the first time. "Jeez, Jess." He took a quick look around. "It's all the odors. Can't you smell 'em? All of this brings memories of the war days racing back through my tired brain like an out-of-control freight train."

He closed his eyes and his chin dropped to his chest. He took a couple of deep breaths, then reached up and wiped a tear from the corner of his eye. "I see the kids, scared as hell, and I hear their cries. Wilson, Ramirez, Swedburg, Washington. And the list goes on and on. I see 'em, Jess. I hear 'em and I still see 'em." He looked at Jesse. "These smells bring it all back. Will the demons ever leave me alone, Jess?"

"Sure they will, Rob. That's why I'm here with you." She grabbed both of his hands and began shaking them. "I want to help you Rob. Okay?" She dropped one of his hands and lightly touched his chin. "Will you let me help?"

He looked at her with a far-off, pensive gaze before his demeanor softened and a small smile appeared. He put his arms around her and pulled her to him in a tight, never-let-go hug. "Sure, Jess. I'll let you help."

She thumped his chest with her index finger. "Okay, then get your shit together and let's go see Clyde. Maybe he'll have some information that can help us catch these assholes."

They walked toward the information booth, and Roberto put his arm around her. "You know, I think I could get to like you, Kid," he said.

"You'd better because I'm not going away."

THE OCTOGENARIAN AT THE INFORMATION booth put her knitting in a basket and pushed her glasses up from the tip of her nose. She stared at the computer screen for what seemed like fifteen minutes before answering Roberto's query. "Mr. Ashburn is in the ICU and that's on the fifth floor. Do you know where the elevators are located?" When Roberto shook his head, the grandmotherly woman took a deep breath and pointed down the hall to their right. "They're at the end of the hall. Just follow the signs and take the elevator on the right. When you get off, take a left and follow the signs.

Good luck and I sincerely hope your friend is okay. We do get 'em better here at Good Shepherd, you know."

By the time they reached the fifth floor, he was perspiring like a lumberjack and his heart was racing like a teenager in the backseat on his first date. He jumped out before the doors were fully open. Using the back of his already sweat-stained sleeve, he wiped his brow. "I hate those damn things too." Elevators reminded him of being in a gook tunnel back in Nam. "Just to let you know, we'll be taking the stairs down. No more rides today." He took another deep breath. "That okay with you, Jess?"

Jesse smiled. "Sure, Wuss."

As he took her hand and looked down the hallway, Roberto was still seeing the smile. He was beginning to feel numb all over.

THE RHYTHMIC BEEPING of cardiac monitors accompanied by the intermittent whooshing of a ventilator told them they were approaching the ICU. After stopping at the nurse's station to inquire where they might find Clyde, they made their way to room 512 at the end of the hall. Jesse's first thought was that Clyde couldn't be seriously ill if he was that far away from the nurses. Roberto was still obviously agitated by the smells and the sounds.

They halted momentarily at the door to peek in. Clyde looked peaceful lying in bed with his eyes closed. His head was raised approximately thirty degrees, an oxygen cannula in his nose, an IV tube extending from his uncovered left arm to a bag hanging on a stand, and a cardiac monitor beeping away at the bedside. Jesse stepped into the room and tugged Roberto's arm to break his inertia.

Clyde opened his eyes and began to smile. "Well, look who's here." He extended and hand from beneath the sheets. "How are you doing, my friend?"

Seeing his active friend incapacitated, but realizing that he was all right, Roberto choked back the emotional tide welling up in his chest. He pressed his fist to his mouth and coughed. "Hey, Old Timer. The question is, how are you doing? Are they taking good care of you, or do I have to talk to somebody?"

"You just cool your jets, young feller. They're taking great care of me. I'm doing just fine, and I'll be out of this place before you know it. Now shake my hand and then give an old man a hug, will you please? And mind your manners, Rob. Who's the pretty young lady you have with you?"

"I'm sorry, Clyde. This is a friend of mine, Jesse Martinson. Jess, meet the old timer I was telling you about. This is Clyde Ashburn."

Jesse walked to the bedside and took Clyde's right hand in both of hers. "It's a pleasure to meet you, Clyde. Rob has told me so much about you. I feel like I've known you for years."

Without releasing her hand, Clyde looked at Roberto. "So it's Rob already, huh? I must say, you do work fast, young feller. Either that or she's really impressionable."

Jesse picked up Clyde's hand and kissed the back of it. "You're much sweeter than Rob told me you were." She gently set his hand on the bed. "Now how about you two get caught up." She motioned to the chair in the corner of the room. "I'll just sit right over here."

"She's a good one, young man," Clyde said. "Don't let her get away."

"Jeez, Clyde. You're going to embarrass the shit out of me."

"Before we talk about anything else, tell me about my Britches. Is she okay?

"We took her to Dr. Trishman in Red Lodge. She said Britches needed a little fluids and some TLC. Should be just fine though, and hopefully I can take her home in a few days. Only until you're up and at 'em that is. I'll keep you posted. Now tell me, Clyde, what you can tell us about the guys who did this to you?"

Clyde stroked his unshaven face. "I was just sitting in my chair reading my Bible when I heard a car drive up. Don't get many visitors, you know. He initially told me his friend was sick and wanted to use my phone to call a doctor. When I told him I didn't have a phone, he asked me for a glass of water. I turned to get him one, and he pushed me into the house. Britches growled and he kicked her in the side. Now I ask you, what kind of a man would kick a good old dog like Britches? I told him I didn't appreciate him hurting my dog, and then he pulled a gun on me. He threatened to kill me and Britches. I'm sorry, Rob, but I forget all the little details."

He rubbed his eyes and then his forehead as if that would help him recall these events. "Pretty soon another man, who I assume was his partner, came in with two others, a lady and a man dressed like a preacher, except with the garb he had on I think he looked more like a rabbi. Anyway, the head guy was a mean old S.O.B. He tied me up with duct tape, and they took my rifle and handgun, some ammo, coats, blankets and food. They stole my old ATV as well."

"Was there anything distinguishing about these guys? Something, or anything that may help us?"

"The head guy, the guy who tied me up and kicked the dog, was real mean looking." Clyde's eyes were darting as he attempted to recall every detail. "Muscular, big arms, unshaven, scraggly hair; short on top and long in the back. And he had this ugly spider tattooed on his neck. Worst damn tattoo I've ever seen. To top it off, he ground out one of his cigarette butts on the rug in front of my kitchen sink." He shook his head. "Sorry, Rob, but that's about all I can recall of that guy. The other guy was a follower, that's for sure. Skinny, short, face was acne-scarred. Kind of weasel-like if you know what I mean."

Clyde became excited and began shaking his right hand. "There is one other thing, Rob. They obviously aren't too smart. They called each other by their names. One, the bad one, is Lloyd and the other is Benno. Hope that will help you some, but that's about all I can remember."

"Thanks, Partner. I think you've given us some good stuff. There will be an officer in to ask you some more questions if one hasn't already been here. Would you agree, Jess?"

Jesse had been watching the interaction between Rob and Clyde. The compassion these two men had for each other was quite obvious. She had also been looking at Roberto and, although she had known him for only a short time, at this moment he seemed most impressive. At the coffee shop she had guessed he carried about two hundred pounds on a six-two frame. And now she could see he was solid muscle. His chiseled jaw sported a rough but handsome growth. The beard, matching his dark hair, was sprinkled generously with gray. His eyes were a deep blue, and the look they cast was the most intense she had ever seen. She thought that maybe, just maybe, she was starting to fall for this guy. Roberto's question had startled her, but she had caught enough of their discussion to answer. "Yes. I agree. I think you've been very helpful, Clyde." She sat up straight and took a deep breath. "So, Rob, where do we go from here?"

"Well, I think we should head over to the Billings PD to see Detective Lindsberg. Then we'll decide the next step."

Roberto shook Clyde's hand gently and gave his dear friend a hug. "You just get better, Old Timer. Believe you me, we will get these bastards." He held out his hand to Jesse. "Let's go, we've got a lot of work to do."

Jesse took his hand, and they headed for the door. She looked over her shoulder and smiled. "See you later, Old Timer."

CHAPTER 24

"Hey, guys, how about a little help here." Brendan Brownlee was smiling despite struggling with a large duffel bag he was attempting to lash down on the back of his Polaris 550 ATV. He absolutely loved the bright red color and thought it looked a lot sharper than the camouflage one the dealer had tried to persuade him to buy. And the power this baby had!

The small trailer he liked to pull behind his ATV was already packed with their tent, cooking gear, and sleeping bags. All their food and clothes were packed in the trailer his wife Susan would pull behind her ATV. Hers was smaller than his, but because she was so petite, he marveled at her ability to handle a machine of any size, to say nothing of this one.

This four-day trip into the mountains was one of the biggest events in the Brownlee family every year, perhaps even bigger than Christmas. This year they planned to spend the first night at Wild Bill Lake. The family had spent numerous weekends camping at Wild Bill Lake and found it to be quaint and almost storybook-like. Brendan had made the camping reservations and arrangements to leave their 2007 Yukon and trailer parked while they traveled approximately twenty miles further west into the mountains for a long weekend of camping, fishing, hiking, and bird watching. He knew from discussions with their friends that it wouldn't be long before their twelve-year-old son Peter and his eleven-year-old sister Vickie would prefer to hang out with their friends on weekends rather than go camping with their parents. But for now he reveled in their enthusiasm.

"Hey, team," he yelled again, "we can't leave until all this gear is packed, so how about a little help." His smile grew. "Or should we just stay home?" He knew that would get them going.

The kitchen door of their three-bedroom stucco rambler flew open, and Peter came running out. "I'm coming, Dad! Can I drive your four-wheeler this weekend? Huh, please, Dad?"

"We'll see. Now, give me a hand with this so we can get out of Dodge." This was shaping up to be a perfect weekend.

CHAPTER 25

During the fifteen-minute drive from the Good Shepherd Hospital to the Billings Police Department, Jesse attempted to make some small talk, but Roberto was lost in his thoughts about the ruthless and senseless attack on Clyde. He was also beginning to formulate some ideas about what he would do to the perpetrators when he caught them. And he would catch them. No law enforcement agency could deny him that.

By the time they arrived at the police department, Roberto had decided that if he was officially denied the opportunity to participate in the manhunt, he would set off on his own. And he was convinced he could accomplish it more quickly than anyone else because no one knew the foothills like he did.

Roberto pulled the big Ford into a parking space, sighed audibly, and just stared out the windshield. Jesse touched his forearm, "Welcome back, Kotter. You were really zoned out there, Rob. I don't know if I've ever met anyone who could shut himself off like you just did. I could have told you I was an alien or there were naked women standing on the sidewalks, or I could have puked my guts out right in your lap and I don't think you would've noticed."

He continued to stare straight ahead for a few moments. "Sorry, Jess. I was just thinking about poor Clyde and the injustices he experienced." He hit the steering wheel with the flat of his hand. "I am going to get those bastards, Jess! No doubt about it." He managed a small grin. "And I truly hope you are with me when I do."

"Hey, I told you earlier that you're not getting rid of me very easily. Now let's go find Detective Lindsberg and have him take us to his chief."

WHEN ROBERTO AND JESSE entered the Billings PD building, Detective Lindsberg was leaning against the counter, smiling at the lady behind the information desk. A placard on the front of the desk identified her as Ashley Gaber. She noticed Roberto and Jesse and nodded in their direction. "You'd better wipe that silly smirk off your face and replace it with your game face, Jon," she said. "I think your guests just arrived."

The young detective turned around, and his demeanor changed. The blush faded and he stood straight, adjusted his tie, and closed the top button on his sport coat. He extended his hand and forced a smile. "I was just passing some time talking to Ms. Gaber until you arrived. She just got out of the Army." His step seemed to have a little more bounce than usual. "Her last tour was in South Korea. Ah, why don't you follow me? The chief's been updated and is waiting to meet the two of you." They began walking down the hall. "Pardon my manners, but how is your friend Clyde doing? Is he going to be all right?" He was looking at the information desk while he was talking to them.

"Thank you for asking, Detective. He's going to be just fine."

"Good. I'll be going over to the hospital to visit with him when we're done meeting with the chief." He opened a door with a sign beside it declaring it to be a conference room. "Why don't you have a seat, and I'll go get the chief. We should be back in a few minutes."

This rectangular-shaped space was the epitome of a cold, institutional room. In the center of the room sat a long metal table with twelve chairs scattered around it that appeared very uncomfortable. One small landscape picture hung, tilted, at the far end of the room. The two windows were covered with white metal blinds pulled halfway up. He looked at Jesse. "Well, at least they saved a bunch on decorator fees."

She chuckled and, before she could respond, the door opened. A man appearing to be in his mid to late fifties, about six foot five and weighing two hundred and fifty pounds entered followed by the diminutive detective. His tie was pulled down and the top button of his shirt was open. His sleeves were rolled up to just below his elbows, revealing muscular, hairy forearms. His hands could have been described as looking like meat hooks. His glasses were nestled in a crop of thick graying hair on top of his head, and he was wearing a smile on his unshaven face. He extended his right hand. "I'm Chief J. Patrick Brennan and welcome to the Billings PD office. Why don't we all have a seat and we'll begin this process."

The chief sat down and began to rifle through the pile of papers he had carried in with him. Detective Lindsberg pointed to the two chairs across from the chief and motioned for Roberto and Jesse to have a seat.

"I think I need to get one thing straight right now," the chief said. "We've asked you here for two reasons and two only. The first is that I want to personally review this case and your involvement with it." He looked directly at Roberto. "The second is because of your knowledge of the foothills and your work with our department as well as with the Carbon and Yellowstone County sheriff's offices on search and rescue missions. We may, repeat, *may* want to ask your assistance in tracking these fugitives. However, the final decision regarding that will not be made until after we discuss it with the FBI agent who is being assigned to this case."

Jesse raised her hand and began to talk, but the chief cut her off. "Just hold on, Deputy Martinson." He nodded. "Yes, I do know that you are a Yellowstone County deputy. If you don't mind, we'll discuss you and your status in due time."

The chief turned in his seat and addressed his young colleague. "Detective Lindsberg, why don't you wander down to the information desk and see if the FBI liaison is here yet." He momentarily softened his demeanor and grinned. "And don't spend any time BS-ing with or ogling over the young lady at the desk. I do see and hear everything that goes on around here, you know."

Within a few minutes there was a single knock on the door, and Detective Lindsberg entered followed by two men, Deputy Thornton and a young man who was impeccably dressed. Judging from his attire, short haircut, and demeanor, the well-dressed man appeared to be a fed. "Chief, the FBI liaison is here as well as Deputy Thornton."

The Carbon County deputy shook the chief's hand. "Good afternoon, Chief. I briefed the sheriff, and he thought I should be here to represent our department and keep us in the loop."

"Good to see you, Matt. Your boss called and filled me in. He told me you'd be here, so welcome aboard. By the way, how's your dad? We go back a long way, you know."

"He's doing just fine, Sir. He said that if I ever saw you I was to extend his regards."

"Well, have a seat." The chief gestured toward the table and extended his hand. "I'm Chief Brennan and you must be the Special Agent in Charge that Clark Benson said he was sending over. I ran the case by him, and he thought the FBI should be involved. But I didn't catch your name."

The agent gripped the chief's hand firmly and smiled. "Good afternoon, Sir. I'm Special Agent Nube Lawson, and I'm looking forward to working with you."

"Well, have a seat and let's get started," The chief sat down. "By the way, Agent Lawson, our other guests are Roberto DeLaCroix and Yellowstone County Deputy Jesse Martinson."

While Agent Lawson was shaking hands with Roberto and Jesse, Detective Lindsberg cleared his throat. "Excuse me, Sir. If I may ask, Sir, just for my own edification, why is the FBI involved?"

"Well, Jon, I called Agent Benson and he told me that with a case of kidnapping, along with the interference with interstate commerce and the assumption that the perpetrators have crossed the state line, and for now we are assuming that is their intention, the FBI likes to work with the local law enforcement agencies until the best possible means of prosecution has been determined. So, I've invited them to work with us until that is determined. Does that answer your question, Jon?"

"Yes, Sir."

"Am I correct, Agent Lawson?" the chief said.

"Yes, Sir, that is correct and that's why I'm here. But please, Sir, Nube is just fine. No need to enhance the moniker with fluffery."

"Well, Nube it is." The chief looked over the glasses perched on the end of his nose. "But I'm still Chief Brennan."

He spread out the papers in front of him. "Let me tell you how I tie the last few days together, and then we'll decide how we're going to catch these stupid shitheads. We know the perpetrators held up the Moskowitz Jewelry store on Third and Buckman two days ago. We recovered some prints and have IDed them as Lloyd Malin and Benno Donnrud. Couple of two-bit losers who spent time in the Utah pen. This Malin character dropped out of high school at age sixteen and ran away from home. His sheet includes things like marijuana possession, vandalism, and petty larceny. He got caught stealing and fencing cigarettes and spent six months in the juvenile system. When he was eighteen he literally beat the shit out of a guy outside a sleaze-hole bar after an argument about some girl. Because the victim did not suffer loss of life, limb or organ, the judge classified the crime as assault with the intent to do great bodily harm with less than murder. However, because of Malin's priors, the judge used the available sentencing guidelines and gave him three to five years at the Wasatch medium security house in the Utah State Penitentiary." He glanced up. "He got out in three.

"While he was incarcerated, the psych staff evaluated him and their conclusion was that he is the epitome of a sociopath."

"Excuse me, Chief." Roberto leaned forward. "Could you please tell an old guy like me just what the hell a socio-path is?"

"Basically it means, in my mind, that he's about as shallow as a puddle of piss on the sidewalk of life."

Nube cleared his throat. "If you don't mind, Chief, I'll take a run at the scientific definition."

"Be my guest, Agent Lawson."

"Some of this might sound a bit textbook-like, but it's important, Rob, you know who and what we're dealing with. So, bear with me. Before coming to Billings, I was living for a while in a small town in northern Minnesota. I was asked by the local police department to assist in the investigation of the murders of two teenagers. The perpetrator, in those cases, was a sociopath so I've had some recent first-hand experience with that type of personality disorder. We have to remember, and try to understand, that no one knows for certain what exactly causes someone to become a sociopath, which, incidentally, is now referred to in psychiatric circles as antisocial personality disorder. Some researchers think it is partly genetic and some think it's partly environmental, and they all agree that it's partly mystery.

"However, the main characteristic of a sociopath is that they have no conscience." Nube spread his hands out in front of him. "Therefore, these people have a total disregard for the rights of others. They don't have the normal empathy the rest of us take for granted. They are unable to feel affection, and they don't care about others. As a result, it's very difficult for a sociopath to sustain any type of relationship."

Nube took a deep breath and pointed at Roberto and then at himself. "For most of us, our lives are influenced by our relationships with others and our love for them. So if you take away love and relationships, what's left for a sociopath? Unfortunately, the answer is quite simple. Their sole purpose becomes the desire to win. They want to win the game, whatever the game may be, and they will do anything at all to win."

Nube stood, walked around, and leaned on the back of his chair. "These people usually have low self-esteem, but they may have an abundance of charm and wit." He held a finger up for emphasis. "And, because they are good observers, they have learned how to mimic feelings of affection and empathy to gain our trust so that they may stab you in the back without anyone ever knowing what's happening." He sat down. "And there is one last point about sociopaths that I think is important. They often have narcissistic tendencies."

Chief Brennan smiled at Nube. "Thanks, Agent Lawson. Well done." He glanced at Roberto. "Any further questions about that?"

"No, Sir."

The chief slid a few sheets of paper aside. "The other character, Benno Donnrud, grew up in a bad home. His dad was an alcoholic who, it seems, liked to use his wife and son as a punching bag whenever he got snot-slinging drunk which, according to the info we have, was almost nightly. In any event, young Benno couldn't make it in high school or in an alternative school, so he dropped out. His high school counselors questioned if some of his problems were the result of TBI from the frequent concussions he suffered due to the nightly sessions with his old man."

The chief peered over the top of his glasses at Detective Lindsberg. "For your…" He used air quotes. "*Edification*, Detective, that stands for traumatic brain injury."

He looked back at his notes. "Young Benno started hanging around with the wrong crowd and got caught vandalizing property." He glanced up. "I find it interesting that the majority of his vandalism charges stemmed from shit he did to the school, breaking windows, graffiti, et cetera. His coup de grâce was agreeing to be the lookout when a couple of his buddies held up, without the use of any weapons, a mom and pop corner convenience store. They heisted some cigarettes and a twelve-pack of beer. The owner hit his under-the-counter alarm, and a black and white was only a block away. Benno was charged with unarmed robbery and resisting arrest. Because of his priors and, again, using the available sentencing guidelines, the judge also gave him three to five years in the same Wasatch medium security house."

The chief slid back his chair and lifted his arms in the air. "And guess what? They became cellmates. And Benno got out in three years as well. The city of Billings became their new home when these two stellar citizens jumped parole after their release."

The chief shuffled some papers around before locating the one he wanted. "Ah, here we go. Anyway, at the jewelry store they took off with the cash bag from the Johansson Brothers armored truck, pulled a gun and shot the guard, exchanged gunfire with another guard, and kidnapped two people before fleeing in a white Ford Windstar van." He looked up. "Just as an FYI, Irving Moskowitz, the seventy-two-year-old owner of the store, died of a heart attack during the robbery. So…" he paused for effect before continuing. "The way I see it, we've got 'em on armed robbery, attempted murder times two, first-degree felony murder in the case of old man Moskowitz, and two counts of aggravated kidnapping. That ought to be enough to put 'em away without a chance of ever taking a breath of free air again. And that's just the first case. Any questions so far?"

Nube lifted his hand off the table. "Chief, what happened to the guard that was shot, and do we know which of the two did the shooting?"

"Good questions." He looked at his young detective. "See, Jon. This guy's paying attention. You watch and listen to him, and maybe you'll learn something.

He returned his gaze to Nube. "Thank God the owners of Johansson Brothers want to protect their guards as much as possible. They have them wear NIJ." He looked at Detective Lindsberg again. "That stands for National Institute of Justice. They are level-three ballistic protection tactical assault vests, and those babies are capable of stopping a 2,800-foot-per-second full metal jacket cartridge. Suffice it to say that his chest hurt a bit, but he's going to be okay." He chuckled. "Probably needed to change his underwear though."

"As for who did the shooting, from the driver's description we think it was Lloyd Malin. He's the bad ass of the two, as you'd expect from what we've learned, while Donnrud would appear to be kind of a squirmy, weasel-like guy."

"Chief," Roberto intervened, "from what my friend Clyde Ashburn said of the two guys, that description would fit perfectly. That's pretty much how he described them."

The chief nodded. "What we need is something to tie the two crimes together."

"I believe we've got that for you, Chief." Deputy Thornton sat up a bit straighter in his chair. "I called our crime scene team and had them come to Mr. Ashburn's home and asked them to please expedite their investigation. They called the sheriff, before I left his office, to say they picked up some prints and ran them through IAFIS, confirming the assailants as Lloyd Malin and Benno Donnrud."

Roberto shook his head. "Can they really get that info back to you that quick?"

The chief smiled. "The average response time is about ten minutes for a criminal fingerprint submission." He turned to the Carbon County deputy. "Thanks, Matt. Good work." He raised his hands and looked around the table. "Well, that puts them at both scenes." He rubbed his hands together. "Now let's see what we have against them at Mr. Ashburn's. Of course we're going to need Mr. Ashburn's complete statement…" He looked over his glasses and pointed at Detective Lindsberg. "Which you will obtain as soon as we are through with this meeting. But the way I see it, I believe our DA would go for breaking and entering, armed robbery, and first-degree assault. Those charges should put them away for at least twenty years."

He pushed his chair back, stretched out, and clasped his hands behind his head. "They've got to know they're in deep shit, so they won't give up easily. Especially this Malin character. Our concern here has to be for the two hostages. How do you see this thing, Nube?"

"I have to admit, Sir, that I don't have much field experience, but from what I know, I concur." He turned to Roberto. "Mr. DeLaCroix,"

Roberto held up his hand, "Please, it's Roberto or Rob, but not Mister and not Robbie."

"Fair enough, Rob. The question I have for you is about the geography."

"Rougher than shit. That's why I do so many search and rescue operations for hikers, campers, and hunters. I think it's fair to say these guys haven't got a clue what they're up against, especially with two hostages." He repeatedly folded and unfolded his hands. "With the trees, deadfall, elevation changes, and mountain streams, to say nothing of the occasional bear, well, suffice it to say that the terrain is a real bitch for the untrained."

Nube looked up from the notes he was taking. "What would you guess is their destination?"

Roberto wiped his brow with the back of his hand and thought for a moment. "If they looked at an atlas, I think they might try to head for Cooke City. I'm not a betting man, but I'll bet you a nickel that they won't make it. I agree with the chief: I think our goal here is to recover the two hostages and let the chips fall where they may for the two, as the chief called them, shitheads."

Nube smiled again. "Knowing the terrain as you do, do you think we should employ land, air, or both for the search?"

Roberto leaned forward again with both arms stretched out on the table top. "Remember I've only done search and rescue for good guys, but my thought here is that it would be best to just do land. They hear anything like a plane or a chopper and it might spook them. They, and especially this Lloyd character from what I'm gathering, might decide the two hostages are no more than baggage to be disposed of.

They might figure the best thing to do is to just off 'em and make their trip easier. I think our best chance, in this case, is stealth if you want to keep the two hostages alive."

Nube tapped his pen on his notepad. "Would you be interested in helping us pursue these, if I may, shitheads, Rob?"

Roberto hesitated a moment. "Who's us?"

"I do believe the *us* is the FBI and, in this case, the FBI is me," Nube said.

"In that case, certainly. Provided Deputy Martinson can accompany and assist me, ah, us, in the pursuit." He looked at Jesse, who was smiling, and he allowed himself a small smile in return.

Nube squirmed in his chair and grimaced. "I'm not sure my—"

He was not allowed to finish because Jesse stood up and put both hands on her hips. "Now you listen here, Agent Lawson. I've got a helluva lot more experience in these foothills and mountains than you have or ever will have. In addition to my training, my daddy has told me since I was a little girl that if a mouse farted in the weeds four hundred yards away, I would be able to hear it, see the grass move, and smell the odor. And furthermore, if Rob says he wants me there, I'm going. End of discussion." She stared at Nube, and Rob chuckled.

Nube shrugged and turned to Chief Brennan. "What do you think, Chief?"

"It looks to me like you have a fair proposition in front of you, Nube. Question is, can you sell it to your boss?"

Nube pointed at Roberto. "If he's the best you've got, and I believe he is from the resume you gave me, the answer is, I think so. Let's say I'll give it my best shot. Do you have anybody from your department you want to send along on this mission?"

Roberto leaned forward. "Let me say something before you answer that question, Chief Brennan." He mirrored Nube's style by pointing at him while addressing the chief. "It's going to be tough enough to drag him along without adding another rookie to the pursuit team. How about you keep your men here and we'll stay in contact via sat phone?"

The chief thought for a moment, then slowly shook his head. "I agree that the pursuit team should be small." He looked directly at Detective Lindsberg, who had leaned forward in eager anticipation of being added to the team. "And I also agree it would be difficult to have more than one rookie out there." He sighed deeply. "And we have invited the FBI to be a part of this. So I suggest that you sell this team to your boss, Nube, and do it ASAP so we can begin the pursuit. But just remember, these guys are dangerous so take all precautions. When can you be ready to leave, Rob?"

"I plan on leaving from my house at 0600 tomorrow. Not a minute later."

The chief turned to Nube. "Well, Agent Lawson, looks like you have your work cut out for you if you're going to be a part of Rob's team."

Roberto stood up and gestured to Jesse and then at the door. "And don't be late. Any questions, give me a call." He slid a piece of paper across the table with his phone number on it and walked to the door with Jesse right behind him.

CHAPTER 26

"Hey, Lloyd, how about we call it a day. My feet are killing me, and the rabbi is getting tired as well. It might have helped, you know, if you had let the rabbi and me ride for a bit."

"Shut your pie hole, Lady. We'll stop when I say we stop." He retrieved his pack of Marlboros from his shirt pocket, flipped open his Bic lighter, and lit the cigarette. He inhaled deeply and pointed at her, mimicking a handgun. Smoke blew out his nostrils. "And I'll decide who rides and who walks. And don't forget it!"

Benno held up both hands. "Hold on, Lloyd. Let's be cool now. She does have a point, I mean about being tired. I'm getting a bit pooped myself. Besides, there's a nice mountain stream right here." He pointed. "And lots of firewood. We can get some good water, make a little coffee, and maybe even cook something hot. Might do us all good. Whadda you say, huh?"

Lloyd slowly shifted his gaze from Sheila to Benno, and a sneer replaced the wild look that had been on his face. His neck began to twitch, casing his tarantula to wiggle. Sheila looked away in disgust, and Benno looked at the ground. God, he hated that stupid tattoo.

The cigarette was bobbing from the left side of his mouth. "You're gettin' soft on me ain't you, Benno?" Lloyd shook his head and kicked a stone toward the stream. "And I used to think you were made of somethin'. But I see now that you ain't made of nothin' except yellow bullshit."

Lloyd crouched and pulled the .44 magnum from his belt. Swinging the pistol to ensure he had pointed it at everyone, he let his arms drop and stood up. "I should just shoot the whole silly-ass lot of you and be done with it. You ain't worth nothin' except a big-ass ol' headache." He used the sight at the end of the barrel to scratch his right temple before returning it to his belt.

"Okay, okay. Just to show you that I'm not the bad ass you think I am, let's make camp here." He crushed the stub of his still-burning Marlboro with his toe and pointed at Benno. "Make a small fire. And I want some good coffee! Not like that shit you made this mornin'. And fry up some of those spuds we got from the old man."

He turned to Sheila and the rabbi. "You two pick up some firewood, but stay close where I can keep an eye on you. Just remember, if you try to run, I'll kill you. It's as simple as that. All bullshit aside. Now I'm just gonna sit down here and rest a bit. Got me some thinkin' to do."

Sheila and the rabbi began searching for some suitable firewood. She motioned for him to come closer. "That Lloyd is one awful, scary man."

"Yes, that he is. You know, Sheila, I do believe it would be beneficial to you and to us if you would treat him with the proverbial kid gloves. A psychopath like him would think nothing of just killing either or both of us. We just need to bide our time, pray, and have faith and we will be rescued."

"What makes you so sure, Rabbi?"

He forced a smile. "Please. Please call me Ira. There's no need for formalities. What makes me so sure is my faith in God. You do have faith in God, don't you Sheila?"

Sheila stared at him momentarily. She couldn't believe her faith was being questioned. "Yeah, I believe in God. I kinda wish He'd throw us a miracle right about now though."

"Hey you two, quit your dickin' around and pick up some firewood!"

Sheila looked at Lloyd, who was sitting against a stump, and muttered under her breath, "Piss off, you dickhead."

"That's just the kind of behavior I was talking about, Sheila."

She shook her head, knelt down, and began picking up a few dead sticks. It seemed like the whole forest floor was covered with them. When she had accumulated an armload she stood. "May I ask you something, ah, Ira?"

"Absolutely, Sheila. Anything you want."

"This is kind of a twist on the 'how'd a nice guy like you end up in a place like this' question, but how did you end up in Billings and how come a sweet guy like you is still single? If you don't mind my asking, that is?"

Ira glanced at Lloyd. "I see that Lloyd is beginning to get restless. Perhaps we'd better get back to this firewood. I don't mean to dodge your questions, and I will answer them. But now is not the right time." With that he began walking toward Benno, who was pacing and looking from them to Lloyd.

Benno had attempted to construct a fire ring from a few stones he'd found along the bank of the stream. A small campfire pot filled with water and a frying pan were sitting off to the side. He rubbed his hands through growing stubble on his chin and pointed at Ira and Sheila. Sheila thought his fingers were so taut they might break. "Jesus, guys," Benno whispered. "Can't you see how he is? You gotta work with me here. I'm not sure I can control him. He's a frickin' maniac!"

Sheila bent down and dropped her armload of sticks. She moved a few stones into the center of the circle Benno had created so that a pot or a pan could sit on them outside the fire. She motioned to Benno and Ira. Ira knelt, dropped his armload of sticks, rubbed the soreness out of his arms, and brushed the dust from his jacket sleeves. Benno was still standing and stealing nervous glances toward Lloyd. Sheila tugged on his pant leg until he knelt down.

Ira was the epitome of calm, but she could almost see and hear the fear oozing out of Benno's skin. "Benno, for Christ's sake, cool it! You're squirmy enough to piss off anyone. Let's just build a fire, cook some food, and try to get some rest. Maybe a full stomach will ease Lloyd's tensions."

"Yeah, maybe you're right. I gotta yell at you to, you know, make it look good for Lloyd. Just don't think I'm pissed. It's just an act. I'll try my best to get you out of this alive, but I can't promise you anything."

Sheila was beginning to think this accomplice was also a victim in this macabre adventure. She patted Benno's forearm. "Thanks, Benno. We know you will." Nodding toward Ira, she began to gently rub Benno's forearm. "We're in this together, Benno. We know Lloyd's the bad ass here and that you got sucked into this thing. We trust you, so you go ahead and do your thing."

Benno stood up. "All right, you two, that's enough dickin' around! You heard Lloyd! Get some supper started! You, Sheila, or whatever your name is, peel some of those spuds and get some of that bacon out! Hey, Preacher Man, get some more wood! We're goin' to need some for the night. And, dumb shit, find some this time that's not wet! We want fire, not smoke. And when you're done, how about breakin' some of those pine branches so Lloyd and I have a soft bed to sleep on tonight." He looked at Lloyd, who was lying on the ground with his hands clasped behind his head and his legs crossed. "Sound good, Lloyd? A little softer bed tonight, huh?"

"Yeah, sure, Benno. Just get 'em to get some supper goin'."

Benno winked at Sheila. She couldn't help but feel sorry for this poor excuse for a man.

While Sheila began preparing their spartan meal of fried potatoes and bacon, she started thinking of the day's trek. They had only gone about five miles because of the terrain. It seemed like the entire forest floor was covered with dead trees, brush, and rocks so Lloyd, in all his wisdom, had decided to follow the serpentine course of this small mountain stream. At least it had provided the opportunity to see some bitterroots, the small intensely white Montana state flower, as well as some bright yellow buttercups that actually appeared as if they had been dunked in warm butter.

"Hey, Broad! I told you to quit dickin' around and get that supper ready!"

Startled by Benno's outburst, Sheila gasped and dropped two small potatoes on the ground. She picked them up and wiped off some of the dirt and small stones, then thought, *Screw it* and threw them into the frying pan. The aroma and the crackling and sputtering of the frying bacon permeated the air, causing her mouth to water.

Lloyd sat up. "Benno, just make sure the broad and the preacher man only get one piece of that bacon and one spud each. I'm goin' to need lots of food if I'm to think straight on how to get us outta here."

"Screw you, Lloyd," Sheila said. "We get even shares or you can cook your own damn meals from now on."

Lloyd stood and turned his head so his tattoo was clearly visible. His lip turned up at the corner, making him look like a deranged gangster. As he approached Sheila he began to twitch his neck muscles, making his tarantula wiggle.

"Lloyd…" Sheila snickered. "I just have to tell you again, that is the ugliest-looking tattoo I've ever seen. Instead of that spider why didn't you just get a snake that was coiled real tight around your neck?"

The crack from the backhand Lloyd delivered to her face resonated throughout their small campsite. She dropped to her knees, but Lloyd grabbed her by the hair and pulled her upright. "Look, Bitch, here's the deal, so listen close. I've just decided that you get jack shit to eat tonight, got it? And when I'm done eating, well, you and me are goin' to have some long-time-comin' needed and deserved fun." He pushed her down. "So why don't you just rest up a bit before the action starts, huh?"

Tears were streaming down her face, but Sheila would not allow herself to cry. She removed her hand from her mouth and looked at the blood. Then she pushed herself up and released a bloody wad of spit onto Lloyd's shoes.

Lloyd stared at his boots and his face hardened. Benno jumped up and stood between them. "Leave her alone, Lloyd. How about if I take care of her, huh?"

Lloyd repeatedly thumped Benno's chest with his index finger. "You piece of shit! Stay outta my way!"

Benno made the mistake of pushing Lloyd's hand away, and before he could defend himself, Lloyd had the barrel of the .38 shoved into his forehead. Benno raised both arms and tried to grin. "Hold on, Partner. I didn't mean nothin'. Honest." He seemed to be trying to force a laugh. "Hell, you know me Lloyd. We go way back. So, ah, how about you put the gun down, huh?" He extended his right hand. "How about we shake hands, Partner, put this little ordeal behind us, have a bite to eat and then get some rest. Big day tomorrow, right?"

Lloyd maintained a piercing stare as he kept the handgun pressed to Benno's forehead. Without blinking he slowly lowered the pistol and used it to swat Benno's hand away. He raised the weapon to Benno's forehead again. "Don't ever get in my way again, Benno. I really don't give a shit if you live or die. It's your choice, got it? Now, get your ass over there and get me something to eat. Then tie those two assholes up for the night, put some more wood on the fire, and let's get some rest."

Lloyd turned to Sheila and the sneer reappeared. "Just remember, you and me ain't done, Bitch."

CHAPTER 27

En route to Jesse's home from the police station, Roberto had given her a list of the gear she would need to pick up for their mission. He was mildly surprised that it only took her ten minutes to pack. Then he stopped at a corner grocery to pick up a few supplies before beginning the drive to his home.

Jesse thought he seemed to be in the same impenetrable state he had been in when they arrived at the police station. She finally reached over and twisted the volume knob on the radio as far to the right as it would go. She happened to catch a rock guitarist at just the moment he hit a screeching high note, causing her to instinctively cover her ears and lower her head, concealing the mischievous grin on her face.

Roberto seemed to rise about six inches off his seat. "Jesus, Jesse, what the hell are you doing?" He flicked the knob to the left, silencing the eardrum-rupturing insult, but he was grinning too. "Guess you caught me there. I'm not used to someone else being around and thinking maybe they want in on what I'm thinking. Sorry about that."

"Hey, that's all right. But it's a little scary when you get like that. Where do you go or what are you thinking about when you retire that deep within yourself?"

He shrugged. "I don't know, Jess. I guess I just get caught up in my thoughts. Maybe it's because I've been living somewhat like a recluse." He glanced at her. "I promise I'll try to stay more in the moment. But I gotta be real honest with you. It might be difficult at times during this venture. It's how I prepared for missions when I was in the Army."

"Like I said, it's a little scary, but I'm okay with that. As long as I know I can pull you back." She hesitated a moment. "Do you mind if I ask you something personal? I mean, something simple, like what do you do? I mean, do you work, or how do you pass your days?" She gestured out the window. "How'd you decide to live out here?" She leaned toward him and laid her hand on his shoulder. "I guess I just want to know more, well, I guess what I really want to say is that I want to know all there is to know about Roberto DeLaCroix. If you don't mind, that is?" She peered out the window for a second. "To be perfectly honest, Rob, I think I'd go a bit bat-shit just sitting out here in the woods all day."

Roberto stared straight ahead and seemed to grip the steering wheel more tightly for a moment. Then he massaged his stubbly chin and smiled. "Does this mean that our relationship has changed from members of the hat box who have kinda become friends and share a passion for ridding the world of dumb shits to something else?"

"Depends on how you answer my questions, Rob."

"Whew. Well, Jess, you asked a lot of questions, and I'll try my best to give you an honest answer." He paused a moment. "I moved here about two years after I returned from Nam. I got back in seventy. There was a tremendous amount of anti-Nam sentiment, especially after the Tet offensive and the My Lai incident. This war was the first time in the history of our country that the media brought battlefield carnage to our kitchen tables every day on the nightly news. We heard about and saw just about every one of the more than 58,000 men and women who were killed." He paused a moment. "And 33,000 of them were only eighteen years old. Like most of my squad. It's unfortunate, Jess, but nobody remembers those statistics anymore. And it was the era of unprecedented student activism. So people began voicing their opposition to the war because one, they didn't like the draft, or two, they thought the war was immoral or illegal, or three, they didn't like the devastation they saw occurring in Southeast Asia." He paused a moment. "The anti-war movement had grown to become more than just a national sentiment. Jesus, Jess, it had become a goddamn global phenomenon! Everyone hated us! And there were all those goddamn rock festivals like Woodstock and the goddamn Grateful Dead."

Beads of perspiration began to show on his forehead and he was gripping the steering wheel more tightly again. This catharsis would be good for him. However, right now, Jesse wished they were at Rob's home, in front of the fireplace, with a good glass of wine. She patted his arm and he grinned.

"Haven't thought about this stuff in a long time." He smiled. "But you asked for it. And there was Bob Dylan with his anti-war songs. Some people said he was telling us the general public had turned a blind eye to the horrors taking place in Viet Nam and that a new method of government was necessary. All the young war protestors, you know, the pot smoking, flowers in their hair, dead heads really bought into that shit big time.

"You've got me on a roll now, Dear." The endearment caught her off guard.

"And then there was Jimi Hendrix. He said something to the effect that the world would know peace when the power of love overcame the love of power or some such bullshit like that. Now that, my friend, helped to fuel the fires of the protestors. And there were guys like Muhammad Ali and all those chicken-shit assholes who declared themselves conscientious objectors. Obviously, that dude took one too many shots to the head. And, Jesus, Jess, all the anti-war slogans that kept popping up such as 'Draft beer, not boys' and 'Hey, hey, LBJ, how many kids have you killed today?'"

He wiped the perspiration from his brow with the back of his shirtsleeve. "And then there was the group of antis who burned their draft cards and then carried a coffin to their local draft board. Now that was a bit much if you ask me. Do you know why we were there, Jess? I'll tell you why. We were there because of the domino theory and Communism, which meant that if one country fell to Communism, then sure as hell the bordering countries would follow suit. And it was our job…" He jabbed his thumb into his chest. "The good old U S of A, to make sure that did not happen."

He paused for a moment. "But I truly believe that a lot of the anti-war rhetoric was fueled by the goddamn liberal media. And they're still doing it today, Jess. The American people wanted and needed someone to hate during the war, and the media was there to satisfy their need." Roberto thumped the steering wheel. "The media's talent was to express the reader's most stupid, ignorant prejudices, as if they made sense, so that the shameful appeared respectable. The end result was simple: people bought papers and watched television. They got what they wanted." He grinned. "I think we have to remember what Churchill said about journalists. He said they are semi-literate cretins hired to fill the spaces between advertisements. Pretty fair assessment, wouldn't you say?"

Jesse laughed. "My father was a great fan of baseball and its history. He especially liked Ted Williams, and I heard Dad tell his friends, on more than one occasion, that Ted once asked a journalist who was giving him a bad time what he would get if he poured hot water over a journalist. When the writer stared blankly at him, Ted said you would get instant shit. But you have to remember something else about journalists, Rob. You should never get in an argument or a pissing contest with someone who buys ink by the barrel. Sorry to interrupt, but I think those two stories are cute."

He looked at Jesse with just a hint of a smile. "I'm getting to why I'm out here, Jess, so hang in there."

"I'm not going anyplace."

"What's really pitiful is that the American public, instead of blaming the government and holding them accountable for our involvement in the war, turned their attention toward the returning veterans who, unfortunately, became the victims. You saw that with all the incidents of veteran harassment, the spitting incidents, the verbal and occasionally even physical abuse, the VFW and American Legion chapters with their World War II vets who shunned the Nam vets saying that the Viet Nam War wasn't a real war.

"Hell, Jess, many guys felt like they almost had to sneak back into the country. There were no parades or celebrations. There were a lot of vets who felt like they had nobody to identify with. I don't know if you know it or not, but there was even a group of Nam vets who tried to give their medals back." He shook his head and his shoulders drooped. "What a goddamn shame."

Roberto appeared to be mesmerized by the oncoming white lines on the highway. Rivulets streamed into his eyes and coursed down the gray stubble on his taut cheeks. The muscles on his forearms grew tense as he held the steering wheel in a death grip. Jesse allowed him his time and then reached over and gripped his arm. "Rob." When he didn't respond immediately, she slid closer and touched his cheek. "It's okay, Rob."

"Sorry, Jess. But you have to admit, it was a goddamn shame."

"Yes it was." She paused a moment. "Let me ask you something, Rob? Do you have trouble forgetting what it was like?"

For a moment Jesse thought he was going to slip into that other place again. "You know, Jess, what I'm wondering is, can I not forget or do I not want to forget?" He shook his head. "There are two things, Jess, two things. One won't let me forget and the other is something I do to not let me forget.

Strange, huh? I've never even told TJ that in or out of a hat box session. So let me ask you something, okay?"

"Shoot."

"Just why in the hell am I telling you these things?"

Jesse smiled. "Because."

Roberto shook his head. "The first is that I have these recurrent nightmares about my last mission. And I'm not ready to talk to you about that yet. The second, and this is the one that I could control, is that I occasionally listen to a Big and Rich song called "8th of November." It's about the day in 1965 when forty-eight guys from the 173rd Airborne Brigade died. Reminds me of my last mission. But I must say it's getting easier to listen to."

Jesse allowed the silence to grow. She thought it would be a good idea to change the subject. "Now are you ready to tell me how you ended up here, or do you want to wait until another time?"

"We've got a few minutes yet before we get home, so I guess now is as good a time as any. I think you need to know that during my second tour of Nam I received a Dear John letter. Like a lot of poor grunts. Absolutely killed me." He paused a second. "Lori Lynn was her name, and I really thought she was the one. She always called me Robbie and that's why, to this day, I cannot tolerate anyone calling me that name. We'd gone together all through our high school years in Duluth and had even talked about getting married when I got out of the service. You know, the typical American dream of the little brick house with the white picket fence, kids, and dogs." He smiled. "All I got out of the deal is a dog."

"Well, as you can imagine, I was filled with anger about the war and how we vets were treated. And I'll have to admit now, I was filled with a ton of self-pity as well." He shrugged. "I gave you the *Reader's Digest* version at the Good Cup, but the bottom line is I started drinking. Couldn't hold a job for very long, or maybe it was just that I didn't want to hold one. I floundered around, left home, and went to Minneapolis, but the story was the same. I didn't do jack shit until one day I looked at myself in the mirror and got real pissed off. I decided that if I was going to survive, and up until that time I guess I didn't give a shit if I did or didn't, I needed to pick myself up by the bootstraps, kick myself in the ass, and get a clean start. So I looked at an atlas and said, 'How about the mountains of Montana?'" He glanced at Jess. "Not a bad choice, huh?"

"Sounds kind of reminiscent of the Texas Rangers in Larry McMurtry's *Lonesome Dove* when Augustus said to Woodrow, 'It ain't dyin' I'm talkin' about, it's livin'," Jesse said. "By the way, that's one of my all-time favorite books. Anyway, I've lived here most of my life except for my stint in the service, and I love it here. So, I'd say you made a great choice." She jabbed his arm with her index finger. "Besides, I got to meet you, right?"

He looked at her and thought that their relationship, at least in her mind, was progressing rapidly. *But that ain't all bad.*

"Now, the last part of the 'This Is Your Life, Roberto DeLaCroix,'" Jesse said. "What do you do, again, if you don't mind my asking?"

"I've just got a hunch, Jess, that the difference between you and a pit bull is that eventually the pit bull lets go. But I'm not saying that that's all bad." He shifted in his seat and glanced at the odometer and then at the roadside. He was beginning to wonder if he had missed his driveway.

"I think I told you that I live what some would call a reclusive lifestyle, but I'm not a hermit. I just like my privacy. By the time I found my property and built my home, I was starting to feel better about myself. And I actually felt like doing something constructive. So I asked myself what I wanted to do. I always enjoyed using firearms. I shot competitively with pistol and rifle in the service, you know." He smiled. "Did pretty well, too. Well, anyway, I approached the county, various law enforcement agencies, and the schools about setting up a firing range, but also a place where I could teach firearm safety. Suffice it to say that it took a while to get the permits, but now I own and run a place, about a mile from my home, where guys can shoot their pistols and rifles. And I teach kids a registered firearms safety course. After a few years I branched out a bit and started guiding a few guys on elk and deer hunts." He shrugged. "Mostly repeaters now. I do all my own reloading, so I do some reloading for a few guys and occasionally I'll do some glass bedding of their rifle stocks."

He sighed. "And I take a few guys a year on some guided trout fishing trips. Found a coupla' nice streams that I named William and Mary. Good producers. Kinda hokey names, huh?"

"I think they're neat names for a couple of kids. Tell me more about the competitive shooting though. That really piques my interest."

"I shoot my Colt Government Model M1911a1 seven and one system for handgun competitions. It's chambered for .45 ACP 230 grain bullets." He grinned. "That baby has a muzzle velocity of 835 feet per second. Now I want to tell you, Jess, that if you thump a bad ass on the chest with that baby he's, as we say, hors de combat.

"You sure you want to hear about this stuff? I mean, sometimes I get carried away when I talk about this, and I have the tendency to get too technical. But, I have to admit, it really gets my juices flowing."

"If I didn't want to know, I wouldn't have asked. Like I said, it really piques my interest. Besides, the opportunity to learn more about you piques my interest as well."

He nodded. "Well, okay, you asked for it. Now my rifle, there's a real honey. I use an FN Herstal Mini-Hectate .338 Lapua Magnum topped with a scope that allows me night vision capabilities as well as day. The sum-bitches don't get away from me with that one."

He pointed ahead. "Well, Ms. Martinson, I've just poured out my guts and laid my heart on a block, and I've never done that before. Not even with Lori Lynn or TJ. But I have to admit, it felt kinda good. But this pour-out-your-soul-Roberto session will have to end for now. My driveway is just ahead. I wonder if we'll hear from that FBI guy about this mission?"

CHAPTER 28

Roberto eased Big Blue to a stop in front of his house. He stepped out of his truck and was greeted by Bogey, who placed his front paws on Roberto's shoulders and began licking his face. Roberto scratched his friend's ears and allowed Bogey to continue licking him. Jesse looked on with a smile and wondered if Roberto would wash his face before she kissed him tonight.

When master and pet were finished with their greeting, Bogey trotted over to Jesse, who also scratched his ears. Winning over the dog would go a long way in her attempt to win over Rob.

"Well, I see that my friend is starting to take a liking to you. Just don't steal him from me, okay?"

"I think we could share him, don't you?"

Roberto shook his head and entered his home with Bogey at his side. The light on his answering machine was blinking. "I wonder if this is a message from our FBI wonder boy calling about the mission."

"Hey, Mr. DeLaCroix. Ah, I'm sorry. I forgot and I apologize. Allow me to start over. Hey, Rob. This is Nube Lawson calling to tell you that my boss, Special Agent in Charge Benson, has approved the mission. And he's also given his okay for Ms. Martinson to accompany us. Would you please give me a call as soon as you get this message so I can discuss a few items with you? Thanks and I look forward to hearing from you."

Roberto grinned at Jesse. "Well, isn't that nice of the FBI to okay my, I mean our, mission. I suppose I'd better give the pup a call and tell him how many pairs of underwear to pack." He shook his head. "This will surely be like taking a babe into the woods."

While Roberto talked to Nube, Jesse took advantage of the situation to peruse Roberto's home, hoping it would give her a little more insight into this man she was rapidly becoming very fond of. From her vantage point, just inside the door, she could see three rooms and another closed door. She was impressed that although his home was rough by nature, being a log home, it was cozy, welcoming, and remarkably clean. The kitchen windows were always a clue to how much attention someone paid to the details of housekeeping. His appeared to be spotless and were outlined with soft red curtains. She grinned. *Nice touch, Rob.*

She walked into the kitchen, which was to her right, and was impressed with how spacious it was. It was highlighted by a small dark stained oak table that appeared to be handmade. It reminded her of the one she had seen in Clyde's kitchen. She rubbed her hand across the top and marveled at how smooth it was. She instinctively looked at her fingertips and noted there was not a trace of dust. The table was placed against a side wall with an oak chair, stained to match the table, on either end. A purple glass vase containing a bouquet of sun-yellow wildflowers sat on the table. Hanging on the wall, overlooking the table, in a simple wood frame, was a print of an outdoor scene with mountains in the background.

Roberto was still talking to Nube, so Jesse walked back past the entryway and into a moderate-sized living room. The far wall was essentially composed of a large fieldstone fireplace with the fire box still filled with the remnants of last night's fire. The smell of the ashes lingered.

There was enough room in a corner, to the left of the fireplace, for a roll top desk. A small framed picture sat on top of the desk. It appeared to be a much younger Rob in his

Army uniform. Some say that it is the uniform that makes the man, but in this case it was the man who made the uniform look good. She stole a glance over her shoulder at Rob, who was still talking on the phone, and thought that time had treated him very well. A shade of gray in his hair, but the body. . .

She walked over to the mantle and saw another framed picture about the same size. This was a picture of an elderly couple. The man bore a strong resemblance to Rob. The oak hardwood floor was stained a shade lighter than the kitchen table and chairs.

Two chairs sat in front of the fireplace. A leather sofa, positioned perpendicular to the chairs, framed the room. One of the chairs was a sturdy rocking chair, and the second was a large overstuffed leather chair with worn armrests and a thinning dark blue afghan over its back. An unstained handmade table, which appeared to be made of pine, was between the chairs. Jesse thought it looked out of place considering the workmanship of the kitchen table and chairs. A crumpled empty beer can and two books sat on top of the table. She was curious to learn what Roberto liked to read, so she walked over to the table. She couldn't help but note that the door to the third room was slightly ajar, and she could see the corner of a made-up bed. The door leading to the fourth space was closed. She had just picked up the books, a world history textbook and a book on wild birds, when Roberto hung up the phone.

"The third member of our team will be here in about an hour. He'll need a bit of time to pack some gear and pick up a few items at his office. I told him we'd have dinner ready for him when he arrives, but I asked him to pick up a bottle of wine. I'm limiting us to one glass of wine with dinner. Tomorrow morning will come very early." He nodded at the books. "I see you found my light reading."

"Very interesting selections."

"I have a genuine interest in history, and I do believe that it repeats itself. Remember when I told you that I guide some hunters and fishermen? Well, in my mind, there are three types of sportsmen. The majority of the guys are really nice and are genuinely interested in having a good, fun, safe trip. Then you have the second group, the self-proclaimed erudites. And the third group is composed of plain old stupid shits." He grinned. "And believe you me, there is a narrow margin of difference between those two groups. So I like to know things to correct the smart-asses and educate the dumb shits." He pointed at the ornithology book. "And they're not just pretty birds; they have names.

"Now that you've looked around, I suppose you have some questions for me." He held his hands up as if surrendering. "Shoot."

Jesse returned the books to the table. "Tell me about the young man in the uniform."

"You want to start with a tough one, huh?"

He walked over to the desk and picked up the picture, keeping his back to Jesse. "I gave you the highlights earlier, but here's some more. I enlisted in the Army right out of high school. I told my parents I wasn't going to college like my older brothers and sisters." He chuckled. "I remember standing so stiff and tall and telling the recruiter that I wanted to be a member of the Special Forces because it was just the right way to get things done." He threw Jesse a mock salute. "Pretty naive, wouldn't you say?

"After basic training it was off to Airborne School and then the rest of my Special Forces training. Man, I was so proud when I received my green beret." Roberto stood straight. "I was assigned to Company C, 5th Special Forces group—that's Airborne you know—of the 1st Special Forces and became a Sergeant First Class. I absolutely loved my job. That's why I volunteered for a second tour of Nam."

He clasped his hands behind his head. "But my life changed forever when all hell broke loose on April 23, during my second tour. It's after that that the nightmares began. Like I told you on the way out here, Jess, I'm not sure I'm ready to talk about that night with you yet. I sure hope you understand."

She put her arms around him. "I'm here when you're ready," she whispered. "Just please don't shut me out."

He returned her hug. "Deal." Then he held her at arm's length. "Now I'd better get busy with our gear. How about if I ask you to begin preparing some dinner for us. You'll find all the stuff I bought for our dinner the other night in the refrigerator. Spices are in the cupboard next to the refrigerator, and the pots and pans are in the oven. Yeah, yeah. Don't give me any crap about that. It's just where I like to put them."

Jesse tried to stifle a laugh. It was her turn to throw a mock salute. "Aye, aye, Sir."

While she began preparing dinner, Roberto made numerous trips to the fourth room returning with items he placed on the sofa. He finally stepped back and surveyed the various piles he had made. He turned to Jesse, who was tossing a salad. "Well, I think this should take care of us nicely. I decided to take essentially the same gear I used on patrols in Nam and when I guide the hunters and fishermen. It's what I call the pack of the bush."

He stood back and scratched his head while pointing at each item. "I've got sleeping gear for us, extra clothes, ponchos for rain shelters, entrenching shovel, axe, trip flares, small stove, toilet articles, gun-cleaning gear, binoculars with night vision capability, ammo, K-bar knife, handguns, and my rifle.

"I'll need your gear so I can pack that. Then I'll get our rations, which are basically going to be freeze-dried trail food and coffee." He smiled. "So you better eat well tonight because it may be a while before you have a good meal again."

She handed him a glass of wine. "I decided to hell with your rules. Enjoy this. By the way, how are we going to haul all this gear?"

"We'll take four-wheelers until we find their first campsite. From there we'll walk and carry. I don't want them to know we're close. Can you handle it?"

Standing at attention, she saluted. "Let there be no doubt, Sir. I think I hear our FBI man coming up your driveway, so I'd better finish dinner."

Roberto and Bogey walked outside to greet Nube and help him with his gear. When Nube entered the house he stopped, closed his eyes, and inhaled deeply. "Oh, Jesse. I can't begin to tell you how great that smells. I haven't had a good meal in such a long time. Come to think about it, I can't remember the last time I did have a good meal."

"Well, you're just in time, Nube. How about we eat before it gets cold, and then we can pack or whatever else it is that our esteemed leader wishes us to do." She looked at Rob. "Do you have another chair?"

"Yes, ma'am." He carried the rocking chair to the table. "I'll use this. So if you two will sit, I'll say grace."

While they were eating Roberto laid out his plans to Jesse and Nube. They would leave on four-wheelers at six o'clock and ride to Clyde's. From there they would follow the tracks that Benno and Lloyd would have inevitably left until they found their first campsite. From that point they would walk and carry their gear. Roberto didn't think it would be difficult to follow Lloyd and Benno since they had one four-wheeler and three people who would be walking.

"Sounds like a good plan to me," Nube said. "Now let me ask you something, Rob. What are your thoughts about what to do when we find them?"

Roberto stared at his wine glass for a moment. "Let me tell you something, young man. They hurt a dear friend of mine in addition to the other shit they pulled and the people they hurt. To me, what they did is the epitome of loathsome psychopathic evil, and to excuse what they did would be contemptible. You have to know and understand something about me. Perhaps it comes from the ranger training I had, but I have this obsession to see evil eradicated."

He took another sip of wine. "I certainly hope those two assholes haven't spent any time dwelling on the art of dying because if it's up to me, when we find them—and we will—I don't give a shit how much they grovel and beg for forgiveness, they're just plain going to die." He finished his wine and looked at Nube. "That clear enough for you?"

Nube stared at Roberto for a moment before finishing his wine. Then he shook his head and grinned. "Well, I think it's pretty clear where you stand." The grin disappeared. "But let me tell you where I'm coming from as an agent of the FBI. You need to remember this is an FBI mission, not a vigilante vendetta mission. And you've been invited to assist with the pursuit and apprehension of these criminals, correct?"

Roberto sat stone-faced.

"Am I clear on that, Rob?"

Roberto finally offered his agreement with an almost imperceptible nod.

Nube cleared his throat. "Like you, I don't give a shit how much they grovel, but we will not just kill them. We will do our best to apprehend and bring these felons to justice so they can stand trial for the crimes they've committed. Unless, of course, they fire upon us first." He smiled. "Agreed?"

Roberto stared at Nube for what seemed an eternity. Then his countenance slowly appeared to soften. "Agreed." He pushed his chair back and stood. "Now we need to help Jess with the dishes and then pack. Morning will come early, I assure you."

CHAPTER 29

Sheila was rolled up, in fetal position, on the hard, bare ground with just one threadbare blanket for cover. But she felt comfortable as she watched the dying fire. She cheered the occasional ember that attempted to escape from the yellow-orange flames licking the black from the night sky. It had taken a while to convince Lloyd that she and Ira weren't going to escape so there was no reason to tie them up. She almost laughed as she recalled staring incredulously at Lloyd and asking him just where in the hell he thought she and Ira would go.

She had looked at Lloyd too many times, but she realized she really hadn't seen him until tonight. When she'd posed the question to him about where they might go in the middle of the night, he'd just stood and glared at her with the blankest look she had ever seen on any human face. It was as if he lacked the ability to comprehend the question. She also noted a bizarre or at least an atypical feature. When he furrowed his brow, a single crease ran the entire width of his generous forehead. She almost chuckled again. It reminded her of a sine wave she had studied in high school physics and math.

She gazed over at this simple but dangerous man. He was stretched out on his back, lying close to the fire, with his hands clasped behind his head, which was perched on a balled-up jacket that served as his pillow. The light, steady snoring indicated deep sleep. Benno, who she was beginning to feel somewhat sorry for, lay close to him, squirming around. The poor man could not find peace even when he was sleeping.

She had tried to tell Lloyd they should secure their food up in a tree and sleep upwind of a maintained fire just in case a grizzly bear should be in the vicinity. Again she almost chuckled as she remembered how indignant he had become. There was no way he was going to accept any advice from "a broad." He insisted the food be kept close to him just so she and the rabbi couldn't take any during the night. She grinned. If Old Man Grizz did show up, Lloyd's indignant ass would be a good appetizer.

Sheila pushed herself up on one elbow and nudged Ira. "Ira, you awake?" she whispered.

He rolled over to face her and waved. "Yes, I'm still awake," he whispered.

"So, how'd a guy like you end up in Billings, and how come you're still single? You promised you'd answer those questions, and now is as good a time as any."

The fire cast enough light for her to see the soft smile growing on his face. She felt like she was seeing him for the first time, and she liked what she was seeing. He was younger than she was, but. . .

Ira propped himself up on his left elbow and looked toward their sleeping captors. "It looks and sounds like they're sleeping soundly." Then he just stared off as if he were attempting to compose his response.

"Penny for your thoughts, Ira."

He brought his hand to his mouth, stifling a laugh. "Okay, here goes. But I think I need to give you a little Montana Jewish history first. The Jews were among Montana's earliest white settlers in the mid-nineteenth century, and we are even credited with founding several of Montana's major cities. We're not really sure exactly how many Jews live in Billings today because not all of them belong to the congregation. Our congregation, I'm happy to say, is holding pretty steady at about sixty members. And our congregation is part of the Reform movement which means, very basically, that we believe Jewish law should be viewed as a set of general guidelines rather than as a set of restrictions and obligations."

Ira glanced toward Lloyd and Benno. "Now, for me. I'm thirty-three years old, and although I've only been a rabbi for three years, I just became the full-time rabbi in Billings about a year ago. I've wanted to be a rabbi since I was a little boy, and the more I studied, the more determined I became to be a rabbi in the Reform movement and serve a small congregation. So Billings was a perfect choice."

He inched closer to Sheila. "While I was in the seminary, I learned that Billings had been without a full-time rabbi since the mid-1980's, so I petitioned the congregation's board of directors, and was accepted, to serve them as a rabbinical student. That meant I came here once a month to serve them. After I graduated from the seminary, I worked as an assistant rabbi for two years while continuing to serve the Billings congregation once a month." He nodded toward Lloyd, who was snoring loudly. "He's even obnoxious when he's asleep. Anyway, following that probationary period, if you will, the congregation offered me a contract. Judaism is different, you know, in that we don't have a hierarchy such as bishops or a pope, so we get hired by and receive direction from a board of trustees."

Lloyd rolled over, passed a large, noisy volume of gas, and resumed his snoring. When he appeared to be settled, Sheila crawled closer to Ira. "I don't care what that… that stupid idiot says, I'm going to add some wood to the fire." She smiled. "Then you're going to finish your story."

She slipped out from under her thin blanket and tiptoed to the small stack of wood cached at the periphery of their campsite. She picked up a small armload of dried and broken pine branches and eased herself to the fire. She carefully laid each branch within the fire ring and watched as the dying fire attacked it like a ravenous dog after a discarded bone. She crept back to her blanket, lay down, and covered up. "You were saying."

"Well, that's basically the story about how I came to be in Billings." He grinned. "As for the second part of your question, well, I guess I'm still single because no one has asked me to marry her." His grin grew to a wide smile. "Yet."

Sheila brought her hands to her mouth to keep from laughing out loud. Despite their present situation she was feeling strangely exuberant, like a young teenager at a sleepover whispering secrets to a friend so as not to wake the other girls. She hadn't felt like this since long before Don left.

Ira softly laid his hand on hers. "Now it's your turn, Sheila. Tell me about you. But before you do, I want to tell you I was impressed how you handled Benno. I think the arm rubbing, 'we trust you' stuff is softening him up."

"I audited a psych class, about a year ago, on the psychology of interviewing and interrogating. I remember this guy telling us that when he deals with a hostile, he attempts to reassure them by making eye contact, making physical contact, and not letting them see he had any preconceived notions of guilt." She shrugged. "I was simply trying to quiet him down and maybe win him over. I think if we're going to get out of this alive, we may need his help."

"Like I said, I was impressed and it seemed to work. Now, it's your turn."

The smile left her face. She began doodling in the dirt before looking up at her new friend. "I don't really think you'd like to hear about me." A small grin reappeared. "Who knows, if I tell you about me, you just might try to steal away in the night to get away from me and not from them."

Ira laid his hand on hers. "I don't think you have to worry about that. Besides, sometimes I like a story with good shock value."

Sheila looked at this man who, in such a short period of time and under the direst of circumstances, was beginning to make her feel whole again. "Well, okay. If you promise not to laugh, throw up, or run away."

He patted her hand. "I promise," he whispered.

"I'm thirty-eight years old, single—actually I'm divorced—and I'm an assistant professor of English at Rocky Mountain Junior College in Billings. I teach a couple of courses on creative writing in addition to my basic English course."

For a moment she felt all of her newfound happiness slowly oozing out of her. But the comforting reassurance of his demeanor allowed her to continue. "I was married to a man named Don for six long, ugly years. He was a physics instructor at the college, but it seemed that his full-time job was drinking. After a period of time that led to verbal and, finally, to physical abuse. So I kicked his ass out two years ago and vowed to myself that I would never be that submissive or vulnerable again. Pardon my French, but that's almost the way it happened. Literally."

Ira patted her hand, "I have heard that word and that expression before, Sheila. Please continue."

"Well, as you can imagine…" She hesitated. "Well, on second thought, maybe you can't, but it's been a pretty boring, unexciting, dull, crappy life since then." A hint of a smile reappeared. "But at least I'm safe. Or I was until we met Bozo One and Two over there. "

"A pretty lady like you shouldn't have any problem finding a new man."

"It's not that simple, Ira. I'm Catholic. That means I'd have to file a petition for an annulment or, as they like to refer to it, a trial of invalidity, with the Diocesan Tribunal. I've researched this, I've spoken to my parish priest, who was supportive, and I think I understand the process. And I truly believe I would have a viable case because of the alcoholism and the abuse. It would cost me $500, but the money is not the reason I haven't pursued it. I believe in the teachings of my church, Ira. And the Church states that marriage is a covenant for life that cannot be severed." She dabbed at a tear forming in the corner of her eye and wiped her sleeve across her nose. "Dammit, Ira, I failed. That's the holdup."

With tears now snaking down both cheeks, she looked pleadingly at him. "Do you see where I'm coming from? Do you understand or do you even believe me?"

Ira slid closer and put his index finger over his mouth to quiet Sheila, whose voice was beginning to rise. Then he put his hand on her shoulder and wiped the tears from her face with his handkerchief. "Yes, I understand, as much as being single allows me to understand. And I believe you. I promise you this, Sheila, when we get out of this mess, and we will, I will do my best to assist you with your problem. As your friend." He gave her a friendly, reassuring hug. He sat up, cupped her chin in his hand, and wiped the few remaining tears. "I have a feeling that tomorrow is going to be difficult."

CHAPTER 30

Brendan Brownlee had been awake since five o'clock stoking the fire, setting out the food they would prepare for breakfast, and packing up some things they wouldn't need that morning. He poured himself a cup of coffee and walked to the lake. It was part of his ritual, whenever they were camping, to have his first cup of steaming hot coffee while he sat by himself at the lakeshore, greeting the new day. This was his time, a time to enjoy the solitude as well as the sense of oneness he shared with nature as she awoke, listening to the birds singing to each other, watching the fog hovering over the lake before being offered up to the warmth of the morning sun, as it slowly inched over the eastern horizon, and marveling at the wariness of the mule deer as they would sneak to the water's edge for their first cool drink of the day.

He was so caught up in the harmony and both the complexity and simplicity of nature that he did not hear his wife approach. She crept up to within two feet of him before breaking a small pine branch. He was so startled he spilled some of his still-hot coffee on his leg. "Jeez, Susan, you scared the crap out of me." Dabbing at the wet spots on his leg, he managed a grin. "And I spilled some of this very hot coffee on my leg. Maybe I can pull a McDonalds and sue you."

Susan put her hands on her hips and exaggerated a child's pouty face. "Good morning to you too, Mr. Grumpy in the Morning."

He dabbed at the coffee stains on his trousers.

"You okay, Brendan?"

His grin grew to a smile. "Sure. It's nothing that a good hug from my bride wouldn't make all better."

She embraced her husband then pushed him back slightly so she could see his face. "Okay, Chief, what's our plan for the day?"

"Well, first we'll—"

Before he could finish she pushed him away. "You get those ideas out of your head right now, oh lecherous husband of mine."

"How'd you know what I was thinking?"

"Duh. How many years have we been married? Now get serious for a change, will you?"

He mimicked Susan's pout. "Okay. Well, the first thing is to try and get the kids up. Then we'll have a great breakfast, finish packing, and head out." He looked at his watch. "I think we can reach Lake Benet by about ten. We'll set up camp and try to catch some trout for lunch. Then it's off on a hike before fishing some more for tonight's dinner." He gave her a slow wink accompanied by a mischievous grin. "After that we'll put the kids to bed and finish our good morning, hi, how are ya. Whadda you think, Sweet Thing?"

"I was with you right up until the end. Now let's go get the kids up."

They walked hand in hand back to the campsite. "This is my job," Brendan said. "It's one of the things I enjoy." He walked over to the tent where his children were sleeping, put both hands on his hips, and said in the most militaristic voice he could conjure up, "All right, you guys, up and at 'em! We're burning daylight so let's go, let's go, let's go! Out of those sleeping bags right now, you sleepyheads!" He allowed a huge smile to creep across his face. Trying to roust his sleeping children out of their sleeping bags early in the morning was almost as much fun as anything else he did on one of their trips.

He leaned against a tree with his arms crossed on his chest and watched as his two children, the pride and joy of his life, stumbled out of the tent. They rubbed their eyes as they staggered toward the campfire where their mother was preparing breakfast. He couldn't help but think that this was going to be one incredible day.

CHAPTER 31

Sheila hadn't slept much after her talk with Ira. She had awakened early and was lying under her blanket staring at the few embers still glowing in their fire. It had been a long time since she had let her guard down and told any person, let alone a man and especially a rabbi, about her life and how she was feeling. She felt strangely good, and she felt like a bond had been loosened and she had taken a baby step toward feeling free and whole again.

She crawled out from under her blanket and folded it neatly. Some habits don't die easily. Ira appeared to be sleeping very peacefully. He did seem to possess a real sense of inner peace. She made a mental note to ask him about that as she walked over to the cache of firewood, picked up an armload, and carried it to the fire ring.

Lloyd and Benno were still snoring, although more lightly than a few hours ago. It wouldn't be long before they'd all have to deal with Lloyd's insanity again. When it appeared the fire would grow, she stretched, yawned, and decided it would be a good time to wander off into the woods to relieve herself.

She had just squatted down to urinate when she heard a branch snap. Quickly pulling up her panties, she saw the outline of Lloyd in the light of the campfire. With her back to the intruder, she stood and pulled up her jeans. "Jesus, Lloyd! Can't a woman even pee in private without you trying to sneak a peek?"

Lloyd raised his right upper lip without letting his cigarette fall out. His neck twitched, creating the impression that the tarantula was moving. He grabbed his crotch and slowly gyrated his hips. "Whatsa' matter, Sweetheart? You afraid I might see somethin' I ain't ever saw before?"

"Lloyd, you are one lecherous, son-of-a-bitch old ogre. Oh, I'm sorry." She folded her hands reverently and bowed. "I forgot that you graduated from one of Utah's most prestigious institutions. I should make that a little easier for you. You are just a dirty rotten old man. And you know what's worse than a dirty rotten old man? Huh, Lloyd? Do you know what's worse?"

Lloyd cocked his head to the side. Sheila had never noticed how big his head was. It seemed about the size of Mr. Doughboy's midsection. Maybe it was because of the buzz cut on top and the long mullet hanging to his shoulders. Who the hell wore their hair in a mullet anymore? And she still couldn't figure out why he had that crazy, stupid spider tattoo.

"What? Is the question too hard for you Lloyd?"

"Whadda ya mean?" He kicked at the ground and ran his hands through his hair. "I mean, what's worse than a dirty old man?"

"Yeah, well, the only thing worse than a dirty rotten old man is a stupid, dirty rotten old man. Like you. Now get your ass out of here and give me some privacy, will you?"

Lloyd took a step back but continued to stare. He slowly raised his hand and pointed at her, his hand mimicking a handgun. "We ain't done, Bitch. Just don't you forget it." He stumbled, which seemed to infuriate him. His voice rose an octave. "You're goin' to get yours yet! Just you wait!" He walked back to the campsite, slamming a fist into the palm of his hand.

Sheila smiled, taking some pleasure in pushing the envelope with this challenged but yet so very dangerous creature. She began the process she had initiated before being rudely interrupted, making a mental note to continue to have her fun, but with careful consideration of what she would say or do.

BENNO WOKE UP WHEN LLOYD WALKED toward the woods. He made a pot of coffee and poured himself a cupful. He was sitting on a stump, sipping from the steaming cup, when he heard Lloyd returning to the campsite. He could tell that Lloyd was already pissed—again. Benno was beginning to doubt many things about his longtime companion. Based on Lloyd's actions and behavior the past few days, Benno was starting to question Lloyd's character and he certainly doubted his ability to lead. Benno realized, for the first time in a long time, that he was afraid. He held the cup of coffee in trembling hands, between his legs, and closed his eyes. He thought he would try to remember how to pray, but it had been a long time.

Hello God. This is Benno. I know I ain't talked to you for some time and I hope you remember who I am. I forgot how I'm supposed to do this, but I guess the reason I'm trying is that I'm scared. As a matter of fact, I'm scared shitless if you know what I mean. I know I don't probably deserve anything, but whatever you can give me, I'd take.'

"What the hell you doin', you dumb shit."

Benno jumped, spilling some of his coffee. "I'm just sittin' here thinkin', Lloyd. That's all. Thinkin' about the day, where we're headed, you know, stuff like that."

"You ain't a thinker, Benno. You're just a goddamn scum bag. Now how about you get your ass up offa that stump and cook up some of that bacon." Lloyd kicked Benno in the foot. "You just remember that I do the thinkin' for us. Now get me a cup of coffee and find me that atlas. I gotta figure where we're headed today."

Benno angrily threw the rest of his coffee away and rubbed his sore foot as he stared at the man he was beginning to loathe.

SHEILA SAW LLOYD KICK BENNO as she walked into camp. She could see the fear and the hate growing in Benno. She knelt down next to him and began to busy herself so as not to upset Lloyd, who had settled into the same position he had assumed last evening. She nodded toward Lloyd, who was lighting another cigarette, and spoke to Benno. "I bet he's pissed, huh? Well, that's my fault. I guess he got upset because I wouldn't let him watch me while I urinated. Let me help you get some breakfast ready, okay?"

Benno nodded and handed her the frying pan. "He's frickin' crazy and I'm gettin' scared!" he whispered.

"Just try to stay cool, and somehow maybe the three of us can get out of this." She nodded toward Ira, "I spoke with the rabbi last night, and we agreed that if you help us we'll put in a good word for you when we get out of this mess. Sound okay to you, Benno?"

He began chopping up some potatoes into the frying pan she was holding and appeared to be giving her offer some consideration. After a few moments he looked up with a doleful look on his face. "Nobody was supposed to get hurt at the jewelry store. You gotta believe me. Me and Lloyd agreed that there wouldn't be any guns. That was all Lloyd's doin', not mine. Why were you and the rabbi there anyway? I sure wish you two woulda been someplace else."

Sheila smiled. "Would you believe that I thought you and Asshole over there were priests? I wanted to ask you when the next Mass was going to be said at St. Marks. And Ira told me he was there to perform a specific Jewish ceremony for Mr. and Mrs. Moskowitz." She shook her head. "Yeah, you and I both wish the rabbi and I were someplace else that morning."

Benno appeared to think about that for a moment. "And you saw me at the old man's place, right? I didn't want to hurt the poor old guy." He gazed down at the frying pan, and for a moment he attacked the potatoes with a vengeance. When he looked up again, his face was expressionless. "Yeah, I'll work with you and the rabbi." He pointed at her. "But you'll put in a good word for me, right?"

Sheila smiled and patted his forearm. "Sure, Benno. Ira and I will tell them how you helped us. Now, let's get some breakfast going before Lloyd has a shit fit. You'd better get him that coffee and atlas he asked for. Go on. I'll cook the potatoes and bacon."

While Sheila was talking to Benno, she was watching Ira, who was standing with his back to Lloyd, his hands folded, head bowed, and lips moving as if in silent prayer. He folded his blanket, which he had been holding under his arm, laid it on the ground, and walked toward the fire ring.

Benno grabbed the coffee pot and shrieked, "Shit!" Shaking his hand he looked up at Sheila. "That sumbitch is hot!"

Instinctively, Sheila reached for his hand. "Let me have a look."

Benno spit on his hand. "Nah, that's okay. My own damn fault. Shoulda known it was goin' to be hot." He used his shirttail to grab the coffeepot and pour a cup for Lloyd. "I better get Lloyd his coffee."

Ira knelt next to Sheila. "What's going on already this beautiful morning? And I must say, if you don't mind, that you look great this morning." He touched her arm. "I enjoyed our chat last night, Sheila."

She handed him a cup of coffee. "Thanks." She nodded in the direction where Ira had been standing. "I enjoyed it too. I couldn't help but notice that it looked like you were praying."

"I was saying my morning prayers, Sheila." He glanced over at Lloyd. "Let me give you a very brief explanation, which hopefully will give you more insight into our history, which I started last night. It is our duty, according to Jewish law, to pray three times a day, morning, afternoon and evening. Each prayer was given to us by a patriarch who served God in a special way. Abraham, who served God with love and kindness, gave us our morning prayer. Isaac gave us our afternoon prayer and served Him with the qualities of justice and reverence. And Jacob, who gave us our evening prayer, served Him with mercy." He smiled. "And that, basically, is our prayer life."

He glanced at Lloyd and then began busying himself by poking at the fire. "The Torah was given to us at Mount Sinai, and it teaches us our way of life in every detail. One of the 613 commandments contained in the Torah is that we must serve God with all our heart and soul. And we believe the best way to do that is to pray to Him." He smiled at Sheila. "And that, in a nutshell, is our faith. It would take a lot more time to fill you in on all the details, but I see our leader is getting a bit anxious."

She took a quick look at Lloyd. "You're right. So how about you get some more wood so we all appear busy. That will keep Chief Dickhead from exploding. At least for a while. And you can finish your lecture later. Always the teacher, aren't you, Ira?"

Ira sipped at his coffee, but did not stand to leave. "Sheila, what's the deal with Benno? I saw the two of you in what appeared to be a serious discussion."

"Benno's in a state of not knowing what side of the fence he's on nor what side he wants to be on. I told him we had decided that if he helps us get out of this mess we would put in a good word for him. I'm trying to win him over to our side." She took a sip of coffee. "And I think it's working. So, my friend, anything you can do to assuage his fears and befriend him will help us."

"Got it. I'll do what I can. Now I'm off to get some firewood for you. You're right in that we don't want to upset Lloyd, but…" He winked and pointed a finger at her. "I don't want to upset you either."

"Hey you two!" Lloyd yelled. "Quit dickin' around and get me some breakfast! My stomach's growlin' from thinkin' too much!"

Lloyd had been looking at the atlas and peering off in different directions. *That dipshit hasn't got a clue where we're at. And he doesn't have a compass. This should be one interesting day.* "Yeah, yeah, hold your pants on, will you?" Sheila said. "It'll be done in about two minutes. Hey, Rabbi, hurry up with that wood! I need to cook on fire and I can't cook on hope!"

Ira had just picked up an armload of dead branches and was walking toward her. He gave her a look as if to ask what that was all about. Sheila rolled her eyes and nodded toward Lloyd. Then she did something that even caught her by surprise. She blew him a kiss. Ira stopped dead in his tracks. His mouth fell open and he dropped the branches.

He regained his composure and coughed. "Oh shoot, I tripped. Be there in a second with the wood, Sheila." He looked at her again as if to ask what that was all about. She just shrugged and continued stirring the potatoes and bacon.

When they had finished eating, Sheila took the frying pan to the river to wash it out while Benno and Ira put out the fire and began packing up their gear. Lloyd was sitting on his stump again, looking at the atlas while scratching his head. He closed the atlas. "All right, you assholes get over here. I'll tell you where we're headed today."

The trio cautiously approached Lloyd, who was using a twig to draw what appeared to be a map in the dirt. They stood before him like school children awaiting their punishment from the principal. After what seemed like an eternity, Lloyd stood and focused his despicable gaze on each person, his mouth open in a sneer revealing his tobacco-stained teeth. Then he tapped the ground with the twig. "This here's a map, best as I can draw, of this area as I read the atlas. Right now we're west and south of Red Lodge. My goal is to get to Cooke City." He tapped the ground again. "Which is right about here." He looked up at the pensive trio. "It's going to be some rough goin', no doubt about it." He snickered. "And I gotta tell you three dumb shits that I plan on makin' it but could give a rat's ass if you make it. You just ain't tough like me, and it's gonna take tough to make it."

He returned his gaze to the map he had sketched. "We're gonna follow this here river cuz I'm sure it'll bring us to a lake somewhere south where we can fish and maybe hole up a day or two. Let the trail and the heat kinda cool off a bit. So we're goin' today until we find us a lake." He looked up and fixed a lecherous, nausea-inducing stare on Sheila. He raised the twig and tapped her on the arm. "Who knows. Might be a nice place for us to take a bath." He tapped her arm again and added with a chuckle. "Together. You know, get the trail dust off."

Sheila grabbed the twig, held it up in front of Lloyd, snapped it in two, and threw the pieces at him. "Go screw yourself, Lloyd." Then she spit on him.

He raised his fist, but before he could strike, Benno stepped in front of him with his arms raised. "Hold on, Lloyd.

If you hurt her, then we got an injured one on our hands to take care of. It would just make it tougher for us."

Lloyd maliciously thumped Benno in the chest with his fist and pushed him back. "I told you once before, never step in front of me again!" He pulled out the .38 and struck Benno on the right ear. "When the hell you ever gonna learn, Benno?"

Sheila seized the advantage to show Benno she and Ira were on his side. "That's enough, tough guy. You got a beef with me, talk to me. You don't have to take it out on Benno."

She tore off a small piece of her blouse and used it to wipe the blood welling up from the small gash on Benno's ear. "Are you all right, Benno? That was nice of you to stick up for me, but you don't have to do that. I can fight my own battles. Now let me get a better look at that wound."

Benno pushed her hand away and looked at Lloyd. "I'm okay. I can take care of myself. Don't need no broad to help me." He tore off a piece of his flannel shirt and began dabbing at his wound. "I had it comin'. I'm okay, Lloyd. I promise I won't do it again." He pointed at the marred sketch in the ground. "I like the plan, Lloyd. We ready to head out, huh?"

Squinting, Lloyd clenched his jaws so tightly it caused his facial muscles to bulge out. "Yeah, let's get goin'." He turned to Sheila with the most evil, hateful glare she had ever experienced. "You just remember, Bitch, we ain't done."

She returned the stare. *You're right, Asshole, we're not.*

CHAPTER 32

Jesse was awakened by the smell of frying bacon accompanied by the sound of grease splattering and crackling in a cast-iron pan. She inhaled the mouth-watering aroma deeply and thought she could also smell freshly brewed coffee. She rolled over and looked at the digital alarm clock on Roberto's bedside nightstand. The bright red numbers told her it was only 4:10 a.m. *Jeez, Rob said we would get up at four-thirty. Well, I'll be damned if I'm getting up yet.'*

She closed her eyes and pulled the pillow closer to her, imagining it was Rob and thinking she could smell him. She found the sensation to be sensually arousing. She'd been disappointed last night when the group was finally ready to turn in and Rob suggested—no, he pointed and said in a manner that left no room for discussion—that she would sleep in his bed and he and Nube would sleep on the couch and floor in the living room. *Well, it was probably for the best.*

She allowed herself a few minutes before getting up and slipping on a robe Rob had placed on the end of the bed for her. She eased the bedroom door open and quietly watched Rob and Nube. Both were attired in their ninja-like tactical assault uniforms and were poring over a map Rob had spread out on the table. He was pointing out something of interest with one hand while using the other hand to scratch Bogey's ears.

Jesse walked over to the table. "Well, look at my two soldier boys. By the way, Rob, I thought reveille was 0430 and not 0400." She closed her eyes and inhaled deeply. "But I must say the breakfast smells really good."

"Good morning to you too, Jess. Breakfast will be ready in just a few minutes. I'd suggest you get dressed because we'll be leaving right after we eat. Nube and I already have the four-wheelers gassed, packed and ready." Roberto looked at his watch. "You've got about four minutes." Then he returned his gaze to the map.

With mouth agape Jesse stared at him before walking to the bedroom. *That's a great way to start the day!*

When she emerged from the bedroom three minutes later, there were platters of bacon, scrambled eggs, and toast on the table with a cup of steaming coffee she assumed was for her. Roberto handed the cup of coffee to her. "I apologize, Jess. I was a bit abrupt earlier. How about if we start the day over? Okay?"

Jesse furrowed her brow and pursed her lips, but could not continue the ticked-off pose very long. She took a small sip of the coffee and smiled. "Sure. Good morning, Rob. Did you sleep well?"

"Good morning, Jess. Yes I did and I trust you did as well. Now, how about some breakfast so we can get going?"

"One thing first." She set the coffee mug on the table and gave him a hug and a small kiss on the cheek. "Okay, let's eat. I'm starving."

Roberto finished eating well before the other two and stood looking at the map, which was now laid out over the sink. Nube and Jesse finished their breakfast and carried their dishes to the counter.

"You look pretty serious, Rob. What's the deal?" Jesse asked.

"Let's clear the table and then the three of us look at this map together one last time before we leave."

Roberto held the map up while Jesse and Nube put the dishes in the sink. He laid the map on the table and poured himself a half-cup of coffee. "I showed this to Nube earlier,

Jess, but I think you should see it as well. This is my home and…" He drew a line to the south. "This is where Clyde lives. I told Nube my guess would be that Lloyd and Benno will initially head west and find this trail that leads southwest toward Wild Bill Lake, which is west of Red Lodge. It's fairly flat, as I recall, so the initial travel will be fairly easy for them. Or at least it should be."

He pointed at another spot. "This is about where I would expect to find their first campsite. From there, if they have a compass, and I doubt they do, it's my guess they will aim for Cooke City. But that's mighty tough terrain even for someone who's prepared for it."

He moved his finger. "There are some small lakes in this area that are connected by a stream that flows from one to the next. My thought is that I will have the two of you stick to the low ground and I'll stay higher up. By the way, Nube, did you bring the two-way radios I asked you to pick up?"

Nube nodded. "I grabbed three of our Motorola HT 1000 two-way radios. It's standard for us to use them, and I think they'll work just fine where we're going."

"Thanks. I agree, and from what I've read, they're great radios and should make it easy for us to stay in contact. Like I said, I'll take the high ground. Who knows, maybe I'll be able to spot something from a slightly higher elevation. I just hope there aren't any campers out there." He took a deep breath and slowly exhaled. "That could add a whole new dimension to this pursuit."

He took another sip of his coffee and looked at Nube. "One more thing, Nube. What are you taking for weapons?"

Nube smiled. "I'll have my Glock 22 .40 caliber fifteen-round handgun on my side. And I'll carry my special baby, my Colt M4 rifle. It's compact, has a telescoping butt stock, and is fitted with telescopic sights with night vision capabilities. I have it set for three-round bursts, firing 5.56x45 mm NATO ammunition. That should work, don't you think?"

"I must say, my young friend, I am impressed and I'm glad you're on my side. Yeah, they'll work just fine." He raised his arms and smiled. "Well, as the old guys say, let's head 'em out cuz we're burning daylight." They donned their jackets and exited Roberto's home, accompanied by Bogey.

The four-wheeler ride to Clyde's home took fifteen minutes. Roberto walked around the house to ensure it was intact and, assured that it was secure, he and Bogey began searching for any clue to the direction Lloyd and Benno had taken when they left with their hostages. It only took a couple of minutes before Bogey became excited. Roberto called his friend to heel to prevent the large animal from destroying anything that might help them in their pursuit.

He found the four-wheeler tracks and the footprints of the three who were walking. He guessed Lloyd would ride and the other three would be on foot. Roberto gave the "stay" command to Bogey and walked back to his ATV. He nodded toward Bogey. "The trail's over there. I'll send Bogey ahead of us, and we'll follow." He smiled proudly. "Should be an easy trail, and he'll take us right to their first campsite."

The trail was easy to follow despite the abundance of brush and deadfall. However, it was more difficult to traverse than Roberto had anticipated. The large amount of deadfall caused the trail to be serpentine, and at times it was difficult to get the four-wheelers over a downed log. They could see spots where it appeared Lloyd needed Benno and their hostages to assist in getting their four-wheeler over a rotting pine tree.

After an hour Roberto called a halt to their pursuit. "Let's take a five-minute break. It'll give Bogey a chance to rest and get some water. How are you guys doing?"

Nube removed his bush hat and wiped his brow with the back of his sleeve. "I'm doing just fine. I must say, though, that this is tougher terrain than I would have imagined."

Jesse stepped off her ATV and arched her back. "I agree, but I'm doing just fine. How far did we come, Rob?"

"Only about a mile so far. It looks like they're having some difficulty with the deadfall. About four miles from here there is a small stream. It's my guess that's where we'll find their first campsite."

Bogey was up and sniffing the ground. Roberto nodded toward the English bullmastiff. "Looks like our leader is ready to go, so let's fire 'em up."

It took two more rest stops and about five hours to reach the small cool stream where Lloyd and Benno had made their first camp. Roberto understood why it had taken them all day to travel this far. He noted the remnants of their fire, the scattered cigarette butts smashed into the dirt, and the disturbed ground where they had slept and milled around. He shook his head. The dumb shits didn't even know enough to attempt to disguise their presence. But he had also noted, during their pursuit, that someone in Lloyd's group had been breaking branches along the trail, perhaps hoping they were leaving signs for anyone who would be searching for them.

Roberto turned off his four-wheeler. "Let's take a break, have some lunch, and then we'll begin our pursuit on foot. Jess, how about if you get a small fire going while Nube and I have a look around." He heard a splash and smiled as he saw Bogey out in the cool stream.

Nube removed his hat, ran his hand through his thick, dark brown hair, and pointed at the ground. "Looks like there was a scuffle of some sort here. It wouldn't surprise me at all if there is some discord in their group. Guys like Lloyd and Benno just don't do well when they're under stress. The pecking order comes into play, and one of them assumes the leader role. And it's not always a unanimous decision."

He looked at Roberto. "My guess is one of them, Lloyd or Benno, will get hurt, and I think it's safe to assume, from what we've learned about the two of them, it will be Benno. He seems to be the weaker of the two."

"I agree," Roberto said. Jesse had a small fire going. "Looks like Jess is ready for me to bring out the food so we can eat. Hope you like long rats."

"Just what, may I ask, are long rats?" Nube said.

"Long patrol rations. Don't worry. It's not as bad as it sounds. Actually they can be quite tasty." He nodded. "Especially if you're really hungry. I make up my own and haul them in when I guide hunters and fishermen. Mine are a modification of the British Issue Multi-Climate Ration Pack. Like I said, I think you'll find them tasty, and they're high in calories."

After a lunch of hot vegetable soup accompanied by a biscuit topped with chicken and herb pate, Roberto handed Nube and Jess a chocolate bar for dessert. Nube drank the last of his instant coffee. "I gotta hand it to you, Rob. This was quite good. And I wasn't that hungry to start. If I recall from last night, the plan from here is to walk and pursue, correct?"

"Correct." Roberto picked up a stick and began drawing a map on the ground. "We're going to be entering a U-shaped valley with some serrated ridges that winds southwest. This stream runs the entire way and enters and leaves a number of lakes. Like I mentioned last evening, I want the two of you to follow the stream and their trail, and I'll take the high ridge. Maybe I'll get lucky and be able to see them."

He drew a serpentine line representing the stream. "A couple of miles from here you should come into a clearing where there is a broad grass-sage meadow and a stand of aspen on the east side. I'll be able to see you clearly, but you won't be able to see me. If you are having any problems or find anything you think I should see, call me on the radio and I'll come down. Otherwise, just keep following the stream until I meet up with you."

He smiled. "This is some beautiful country, so make sure you take some time to appreciate it. You're going to see some Engelmann spruce, lodgepole pine, and Douglas fir trees as well as numerous wildflowers, including buttercups, shooting stars, the bright red Indian paintbrush, and my favorite, the bitterroot, which is the Montana state flower. It's a small, low plant with a white to pink flower, so you may have to look carefully to see one."

He stood up and stretched. "Now if you two pups are ready to try and keep up with the old man, let's get moving."

It took about five minutes to tear down their camp and repack their carry bags. Then, with a small wave, Roberto began the trek to the top of the ridge, and Nube led Jesse along the banks of the stream where they could readily see the tracks of the four-wheeler in the soft earth.

CHAPTER 33

Sheila sat on a decaying pine log and removed her boots. She hadn't thought Lloyd was ever going to let them stop for a rest. Her feet and her back were killing her. As she began massaging her aching feet, she was thankful that the elderly man Lloyd had beat up and robbed had suggested she take his wife's old boots. She wouldn't have made it walking in the flats she was wearing when the two assholes decided to make her a part of this venture. As Sheila continued massaging her feet she couldn't help but think, however, that the poor old lady was certainly thinking more of cost than comfort when she purchased this pair of boots.

She pulled the boots back on, laced them tightly, and then sat up and arched her back. She started to massage the kinks out of her aching back. Ira stood off to the side with his head bowed, eyes closed, and hands folded at his belt. His lips were moving in what she assumed was silent prayer.

She smiled as she thought about their middle of the night talk. What a kind, gentle man he was. Was she beginning to have feelings for him? Or was it just that being stuck together and held as prisoners by an insane idiot and his simpleton accomplice had forced her to find comfort in his company?

"Hey, Preacher Man!" Lloyd yelled. "Whatcha doin'?" He began to snicker. "You really think whispering that mumble jumble is goin' to help you? Well, if that's the case, throw one in for me and you may as well throw one in for Benno while you're at it. That poor shit could really use someone in his corner."

Ira grinned at Lloyd and continued his prayers in silence.

The smile left Lloyd's face and his upper lip lifted in a snarl. "You better throw in a bunch for the bitch, Preacher Man, cuz she's really goin' to need 'em. Remember, I said we ain't through and I mean it. It's you and me tonight, Bitch." Lloyd's neck was twitching, making his tarantula wiggle. He grabbed his crotch and began to gyrate his hips.

"Go screw your spider, you stupid asshole."

BENNO WAS SQUATTING ON HIS haunches drawing in the dirt with a large stick when Lloyd began his tirade. He stared at Lloyd and wondered for the hundredth time in the past two days what had happened to this man he'd thought was his friend. How was he going to get out of this mess? If he was going to have any chance, it would have to come through being nice to Sheila and the rabbi.

Benno watched Lloyd carefully after Sheila's last re-mark, especially when Lloyd began walking toward her. *This ain't goin' to happen again. He's not goin' to hurt her if I have anything to say or do about it.*

Benno stood and broke the stick he was holding over his knee. The crack, which sounded like a pistol shot, startled the other three. Gripping a piece of the stick in each hand, he stared at Lloyd. "Hold on, Lloyd. You ain't goin' to hit her again. There's no need for that."

Lloyd stopped and turned toward Benno. A malicious smile creased his face. He took the cigarette that he had just lit out of his mouth and flicked it to the side. "Well, well. Look who just grew a pair." He began walking toward his partner. "Now just what in the hell has got into you, little man?"

"Nothin' got into me. It's just that there's no need to be mean to these people. They didn't ask to come along, and they didn't do nothin' wrong. That's all." He dropped his head and shrugged. "Let's just treat 'em nice for a change. Can't hurt, you know. Besides, she's helpin' us cook."

Lloyd stood in front of Benno for a moment, then suddenly grabbed Benno's shirt and jerked him with such force that his head snapped forward. Benno could see, smell and almost taste the hatred and anger exuding from every pore of Lloyd's body.

Lloyd backhanded Benno across the face. The sound of bone splitting soft tissue resonated throughout the quiet of the forest. As Benno's head twisted to his left, the blood that flew from the reopened wound splattered on Lloyd's face. Lloyd grabbed the .38 handgun from his belt and pushed the muzzle into Benno's left nostril with such force that the blade-like front sight ripped his nose, creating another open wound spurting blood.

Sheila's scream assailed the renewed quiet of their site. She ran at Lloyd while continuing to scream. She began striking him repeatedly in the back but Lloyd, who was pushing Benno toward a tree, was oblivious to her assault. When he had Benno pinned against the bark of a tall white pine, he pulled the pistol out of Benno's nose and swung around, striking Sheila in the face and knocking her to the ground. He raised the handgun and fired at her. The bullet struck the ground just above her head. Sheila stopped screaming and rolled onto her side with her hands in front of her face.

Benno seized the moment to push Lloyd away, but Lloyd swung around and fired a shot that creased Benno's scalp, creating yet another open, bleeding wound and causing Benno to crumple to the ground.

"Lloyd!"

The gentle yet commanding tone caused Lloyd to halt the violent attack on Sheila and Benno. He slowly turned toward the voice and saw Ira standing with his hands held up. "Lloyd. Please stop the violence. There's no need to injure them any more than you have." He gestured toward the two on the ground, Sheila, sobbing and rolled into the fetal position, and Benno, lying unresponsive. "Please allow me to help them," he pleaded.

Lloyd stared at this man he had come to tolerate with no feelings of sympathy or hatred. He slowly lowered the handgun and returned it to the space between his jeans and belt. He looked at Sheila and then at his longtime friend Benno. The expression of pure rage gradually resolved and was replaced by a look of emptiness. He looked at Ira again and regained his usual demeanor. "Sure. Why not. What the hell. In a minute."

He turned toward Benno, who was still lying unresponsive. He leaned down, snickered, and spit on him. "You little puke. That'll teach ya, you piss-poor excuse of a man. I told you not to interfere. You just never learned who the brains of this outfit was, did you?"

Then he turned to Sheila, who began sobbing more loudly and rolled into a tighter ball. "Please don't hurt me anymore!"

"I just don't know why I have these feelings for you, you Bitch." He kicked some dirt on her. "But just you remember, we're not done. Not by a long shot."

Lloyd began softly whistling as he walked away. "Okay, Preacher Man. They're all yours for now. But I wanna move outta here in about half an hour, so you better work some magic on them two." He chuckled and resumed whistling as Ira made his way to Sheila.

Ira knelt down and stroked Sheila's face and hair. Then he lifted her to a sitting position and held her in his arms, reassuring her that she was okay and he would take care of her. The river of her emotions—fear, anger, hatred and uncertainty—which had flooded its banks, was now slowly but surely easing itself back within its confines, guided by Ira's soft touch and reassuring voice. She could feel herself melting into the strength of this quiet, loving man. She could not recall when she had felt so afraid and yet so safe as she did in Ira's arms. Her sobbing diminished to a steady rain of tears. "Please don't let him hurt me, Ira. Please." She leaned up and kissed him lightly on the cheek before burying her face in his chest.

Ira held Sheila tighter. "I won't. Trust me, I won't." At that moment he became aware of an emotion he had never experienced. He wasn't sure what it meant or how to handle it, but he was sure of one thing—he knew he liked it.

Ira removed his handkerchief from his back pocket and gently wiped away Sheila's tears and then dabbed at the wound on her face. He felt reassured that it was just an abrasion and would heal without scarring.

When Sheila's crying had subsided, he took her chin in his hand and smiled as tenderly as he could. "You're going to be just fine. Now how about we try and help Benno. I'm not so sure about him."

Sheila took the handkerchief from Ira, wiped her eyes, and blew her nose. A small smile formed as she looked up at him and touched his cheek. "Thank you, Ira." She stood up. "Let's look at Benno."

Benno was still bleeding from his three wounds, especially from the large cut on his right cheek where Lloyd had struck him with the back of his hand. Sheila dabbed at the wounds with Ira's handkerchief. When the blood was cleared, she could see his right cheekbone. She pressed the handkerchief against the wound to stem the bleeding and looked at Ira. "Hold this, please."

Recalling the first aid she had been taught in a physical education class, she opened Benno's eyes to check his pupils and then checked his pulse. "I think he's in shock, Ira. He's unresponsive even to pain, his pulse is faint and thready, his breathing is shallow, and he's had an obvious head injury. There's no way he can be moved safely now. We'll have to ask Lloyd if he'll give us more time before we leave."

"I'll go ask him. I'd suggest you say a quick prayer though."

Ira walked over to Lloyd, who was lying on his back with his head propped up on a small log. A freshly lit cigarette dangled from the corner of his mouth and his forearm covered his eyes. "Lloyd, can I speak to you for a moment? It's about Benno."

Lloyd continued to doodle in the ground, with the stick he held in his right hand, before slowly removing the arm covering his eyes. "So what's the problem with the little dickhead now?"

"Sheila has assessed him, and she thinks he's in shock and it's not safe to move him at this moment. We're asking you to give us more time before we leave. Just to make sure Benno will be okay."

Lloyd shook his head and threw the stick away. He slowly rose and walked toward Sheila, who had rolled Benno onto his back and was still tending to the bleeding wounds. "So the preacher man tells me that my little dickhead buddy doesn't want to travel. What's the deal?"

"He's obviously been severely injured, Lloyd, and I don't think it's safe for him to travel yet. He's still unresponsive and I think he's in shock."

"Well, maybe he needs a little encouragement." He kicked Benno in the crotch and laughed. "Probably won't hurt you anyway cuz you never had no set."

His demeanor immediately changed as his eyes partially closed and the single sine wave-like crease in his forehead became more pronounced. He took the .38 Ruger from his belt, cocked the hammer, and pointed it at Benno.

"Nooooo!" shrieked Sheila.

Lloyd turned the handgun toward Sheila. "I just might enjoy this as much as I was going to enjoy tonight."

Ira stood up and raised his hands. "Lloyd, if you have any sense of decency. . ."

Lloyd continued to stare at Sheila. He gradually lowered the weapon and released the hammer. He shifted his gaze to Benno and threw the .38 at him. The pistol landed on Benno's abdomen. He started chuckling again and turned to Ira and Sheila. "You can't say I don't care about him. At least I left him a weapon so he can defend himself."

He squatted down and inhaled deeply from his cigarette. He blew the smoke toward Benno and extinguished the cigarette on Benno's forearm. "Just wanted to leave my little buddy a remembrance of me. Now let's get the hell outta here. Now!"

As he walked toward the four-wheeler, whistling, he drew the .44 magnum from his belt. Ira reached for Sheila's hand and the two of them, with one last look at Benno, followed their captor.

CHAPTER 34

Brendan always loved the moment they exited the woods and he was rewarded with his first glimpse of the deep blue lake that sprawled across the valley's floor. *This is it. This is where we'll be camping for the next three days.* He stopped his four-wheeler and sat quietly while he stared at the majestic, intoxicating beauty that lay before him. He was sure this was where God had set his easel when He created this tapestry. The endless, dense stand of lodgepole pines surrounded the pristine mirror-like lake he knew to be so clean he felt secure in drinking its water, without boiling it, or swimming in it without fear. The air was so pure that when he inhaled deeply he could almost imagine it cleansing every cell in his body. This place, unlike any other, was heaven on earth.

"This is it, guys," Brendan said. "This is as far as the trail goes and where we'll be camping. Just look at it! Isn't it the prettiest sight you've ever seen? Other than your mother, of course. Just close your eyes for a moment and take a deep breath. Let it cleanse your soul."

"Ah, Dad. Let's just go. You say the same thing every time we come here. I want to go swimming."

Peter echoed his sister's protest. "And I want to go fishing and catch some trout like we did last year. Let's just get down there, Dad."

Brendan gazed at his wife, who just shrugged. "Majority rules, my love. Let's go."

Brendan released a loud sigh, started his ATV, and waved his arm in a "follow me" motion. The trail down was a switchback because it was too steep to go straight down. He decided the decline would be more gradual than the trail just to show he was in control. Besides, he liked the view.

When they reached the bottom, Brendan and Susan pulled their ATVs into a small area on the northeast edge of the lake. While they set up the tents, placed rocks to make a fire ring, and stowed their other gear, Vicki and Peter put on their swimming suits and rushed to the lake. Brendan watched with a smile as they frolicked in the cool mountain water. He walked over to Susan and put his arm around her. "Just doesn't get any better than this, does it?" He gave her a tight squeeze. "Well, not quite, but then, the day's not over, huh?"

She pushed him away. "We've still got a lot of work to do, Buddy, so you better get busy."

He chuckled as he walked away, thinking he needed to get out the fishing rods and catch something for their supper, otherwise it would just be fried potatoes and beans tonight. Later they'd make some s'mores and then he'd play his harmonica for the family before retiring for the night. Tomorrow would be an active day as he had a long hike planned for them.

CHAPTER 35

The excessive deadfall made the walk along the ridge tough, but Roberto still found it enjoyable as the panoramic view was outstanding. He was able to watch Nube and Jesse, but he was sure they were only able to see him occasionally. He paused frequently to survey the ridge and the river bottom ahead with his binoculars but did not see anything of Lloyd and Benno or their hostages.

He had stopped for a drink of water from his canteen and to scope out the river bottom again when he heard a low growl roll from Bogey's chest. Roberto lowered his binoculars and watched Bogey as he sniffed and pawed the ground. With a soft whistle to get his attention, Roberto gave his canine partner the "sit" command. "What's got you so all riled up here, big guy? Let's take a look."

He squatted down and brushed some leaves aside, revealing bear scat that was still soft. Next to it was a clear, elongated paw print with two full nail impressions he estimated at about three inches. Judging by the size and shape of the print, this was a large male grizzly, and he was close. Pushing his cap back onto his head, Roberto let out a long audible breath. "This, my friend, is trouble. We've got a grizzly in the area." He stood up and scratched Bogey's ears. "We'd better head down the hill and set up camp for the night. This poses another problem for us, boy."

Roberto checked his watch—1600. He called Nube on the Motorola HT 1000 two-way radio to update him and said he was on his way down. He marked the spot and began the trek down the hillside, knowing he'd be back up after dark to look again with his night-vision binoculars.

When he reached the bottom, Nube and Jesse had already selected a campsite close to a rushing section of the mountain stream. He filled them in on what he had found at the top of the ridge and told them they would need to set up some perimeter fires to protect them from the grizzly. He scratched Bogey's ears and smiled. "But we've got the best warning system we could have right here. I remember this spot from guiding. The first time I guided some trout fishermen, we stopped here. Found an old whiskey bottle, so I named this Whiskey River." He smiled at his own little attempt at humor. "Well, we'd better gather some firewood for our main fire and the three perimeter fires, and then we'll eat. I've got a gourmet meal planned for tonight."

After the three of them had gathered enough firewood for the night, Roberto made a fire ring with some rocks he'd found along the bank of the rushing stream. It didn't take him long to have a fire blazing and their evening meal cooking. When they had finished eating their tomato soup, hamburger and beans with biscuits, and chocolate pudding for dessert, they settled back against some small logs they had dragged in and sipped hot coffee. Nube held his cup up in a toast. "I must say, Rob, that tasted delicious." He glanced at Jesse. "You'll make someone a good wife someday."

Roberto chuckled and dared steal a look at Jesse. In the light of the campfire, her short dishwater-blonde hair appeared brighter and her steel-blue eyes seemed to pull him in and hold him. But he also thought he detected a hint of a blush on her cheeks following Nube's remark. She caught Roberto looking her way, and her smile lit up the night brighter than a full harvest moon.

"Well if it's because of my cooking talents, or lack of same, perhaps that's why I'm still single. What about you Nube? What's your history? How'd you end up in Billings?"

Nube gazed at his feet for a moment and walked to the fire where he poured himself another cup of coffee. He kicked an imaginary stone before sitting down. "I guess I owe it to you to at least try and tell my story. You should know, I guess, who you're traveling with. I grew up in the Washington, D.C., area, the oldest of three children. My dad was a family doc, and my mom was a stay-at-home mom. We were a great family."

He picked up a small stick and began doodling in the dirt. "I'm a graduate of Georgetown University, undergrad and law school. After law school I joined the FBI, and my first assignment was in the Washington, D.C., office. I'd been an agent for three years and was awaiting my next appointment. My goal was to become a profiler, much to my wife Ellie's displeasure. She was four months pregnant with our first child at that time. She was driving into New York City to visit a girlfriend when the accident occurred." He coughed to choke back a sob. "She and our baby were killed."

He picked up a stone and threw it into the river before sitting down again. "After that I moved to a small place called Oak Ridge, in northern Minnesota, and worked for a friend of mine at a golf course named Burnt Wood. Strangely enough, I kinda liked golf course maintenance work. Unfortunately, a couple of teenagers were murdered and left in a gravel pit. The town's chief of police—interesting fellow with an interesting name, Naldie Bushmiller—his deputy, Pete Mohr, and a retired doctor by the name of Doc Allen asked me to assist them with the murder investigation.

"I checked with my boss at the time, Special Agent Allessandra Corrales, and she gave me the okay. During the course of our investigation, I met a young Iraqi war widow by the name of Nancy Jameson and her son PJ." He smiled. "I really got to like them."

He took another sip of his coffee. "The perp kidnapped young PJ, but fortunately we were able to catch the perp and save PJ. After that I was faced with a tough decision: stay in Oak Ridge and continue my life at the golf course, and probably with Nancy and PJ, or return to Washington, D.C., and resume my FBI career."

He took a deep breath. "Obviously, I chose the FBI. But believe you me, I've second guessed that decision more than a few times."

"Have you had any contact with this Nancy Jameson?" Jesse asked.

"Initially we called or sent letters two to three times a week, but I've only heard from her once in the last six weeks."

"Where is this Oak Ridge, Nube?" Jesse asked.

"It's about forty miles west of Duluth, why?"

"What did you say this young lady's name was?" Roberto asked.

"Nancy Jameson. Why do you ask?"

"Did she ever tell you what her husband's name was?"

"Yes she did, as a matter of fact. His name was Staff Sergeant Joseph Jameson, and she called him JJ." He looked from Roberto to Jesse. "Now what's the deal with all the interest in this lady, if I may ask?"

"Take it easy Nube. No need to get excited. This is just weird, that's all. I've been attending a post-traumatic stress disorder clinic for years now in Billings. That's where I met Jess. Well, anyway, there's this double amputee by the name of Sergeant Lowell, who told us the other day that he lost his legs when an IED exploded killing his best friend, whose name just so happened to be Staff Sergeant Joseph Jameson. Just seems mighty coincidental, that's all."

Jesse looked at Nube. She could sense that this tall, muscular, well-composed man had a very tender inside. "Do you miss Nancy, Nube?"

Nube dropped his head for a moment and then slowly raised it. A tear eased its way out of the corner of his eye. He nodded and wiped his nose with his sleeve. His voice cracked as he spoke. "Yes. Yes I do. Very much." He stared off momentarily. "I'll never forget the first time I saw her. She had the warmest smile I think I have ever seen. Her long auburn hair was pulled up and held in a flip at the back of her head with a big silver pin of some sort." He smiled. "And her eyes. They were blue, soft and, without a doubt, captivating. I remember I had difficulty talking. I'd like to think I'm cool and composed in stressful situations, but she reduced me to a stammering wreck. I couldn't even order a beer." He continued smiling and stared at the fire.

"I guess there's something I don't understand, Nube. God handed you a second chance and you left. Why?"

"That's a good question, Jess. I liked the FBI and have told myself way too many times that's the reason I left Oak Ridge." He shrugged. "The honest part of me says that I still missed Ellie. But I was really starting to like Nancy. Perhaps I was scared and confused, and I didn't know how to deal with it." He stood up and threw the remainder of his coffee into the fire. "I guess the best answer, Jess, is that I really don't know. I'm a great problem solver, Jess. I really am. But I didn't know how to solve my own problem or where to even begin, so I just left. Quite a man, huh?"

Jesse walked over to Nube and gave him a hug. "Maybe when we're through with this mission, the three of us and Bogey, of course, should take a road trip to Oak Ridge. I've never been to Minnesota, but I hear it's beautiful."

Nube smiled at her and touched her shoulder. "Thanks. I think that's a great idea. But we'll have another passenger.

I'll have to take my German shorthair, Ms. Abby. PJ would be very upset if I showed up without her." He pointed at Roberto and Jesse. "Well, I told you my story. Now it's your turn." He looked at Jesse. "How about you? What's your story?"

Jesse stared at him for a moment. "I guess that's fair. My story is short. My parents were both in law enforcement and my two brothers, well, let's just say that they're still trying to find their niche in life. I guess I could never figure out if we were functionally dysfunctional or dysfunctionally functional." She shrugged and raised her arms with palms up. "That's about it for the Martinson clan."

Nube nodded at Rob.

"It's pretty simple," Rob said. "My parents were disciplinarians. They always told us to never screw up and, if we did, to admit it. Then my dad would add that we'd better remember that whenever the authorities were done with us it would be his turn. Then he'd cock his head to the side and smile. I never forgot the message, and I can still see that smile."

Nube glanced at his watch. "You'll have to excuse me for a few minutes. I have to check in with Agent Benson."

Nube grabbed his Iridium 9555 sat phone and walked away from the campfire. Roberto and Jesse cleaned the dinner dishes and began securing their food overhead, in a basket sling, using a rope over a branch. They were just finishing securing the rope when Nube walked to the fire. "Ah, I just checked in with my boss. I'm afraid he had, ah, had some bad news, Rob. It's about your friend Mr. Ashburn. It seems that he had a setback today. Apparently the docs think he had what they call a pulmonary embolus, or a blood clot to the lung. He's in the ICU now, and Benson said he's in critical but stable condition. I'm supposed to call him in the morning, before we leave, for an update." He put his arm on

Roberto's shoulder. "I'm sorry, Rob. I know how much this man means to you."

Roberto dropped his head momentarily and then looked at Jesse and Nube. He picked up a small log from the woodpile and swung it like a baseball bat, striking a tree. Then he threw it as hard as he could into the still of the night. He squatted on his haunches and held his head in his hands, rocking back and forth, while Nube and Jesse gave him his time and space. Then he stood and took a deep breath.

"No, Nube. You have no idea how much that old man means to me, but thanks for the thought." He kicked a stone toward the fire. "I don't know why I thought of this right now, but I remember reading somewhere that a philosopher once wrote that every man, at some time, asks himself the question, when I die will anyone cry?" He picked up a small stick and threw it into the fire. "Well, I can answer that question for those assholes…" He gazed to the south. "There ain't anybody going to cry for you boys!" he yelled.

He turned back to Nube and Jesse. "You guys take care of camp, please. I'm going back on the ridge and use my night binoculars. Remember to stoke up the perimeter fires before you turn in." He picked up his backpack and walked into the darkness.

CHAPTER 36

Ira had his arm around Sheila as they walked behind Lloyd. Although the terrain was becoming more difficult to traverse, with boulders of varying sizes along the stream's edge, Lloyd insisted on riding the four-wheeler. Ira thought it comical, in a perverse sort of way, to watch Lloyd, with all his machismo, get bounced around like a rookie on a bronco. But Lloyd had informed his hostages that, unless they wanted to carry the supplies, he was riding and they were walking. End of discussion.

Ira thought Sheila needed moral support more than physical support. She would still let out an occasional sob and dab at her tears, but the ankle that Lloyd had kicked didn't seem to bother her. Ira had held the hands of numerous friends and members of his congregation when they were experiencing a particularly tough time, but this was different. This was personal, and this was tough duty because he wasn't sure exactly what he should do. Should he just continue to walk with his arm around her, or should he talk? If he talked what should he say? He was beginning to like this lady very much, and that added a whole new dimension.

He moved his hand from her shoulder to her hair and marveled at how soft it felt. He could not recall ever feeling a woman's hair before, at least not this way. Although it was snarled, he was positive it was the softest thing he had ever felt. Or maybe it was her face. When he had stroked her face earlier, a sensation that he had never experienced had rushed through his body. He smiled remembering how he had enjoyed that strange new feeling.

He leaned over, closed his eyes and smelled her hair. It was intoxicating! A smile spread across his face. Later he could not recall what made him do it or why he did it, but he kissed the top of her head. Startled at this impulsive move, he almost tripped and fell as he moved away from Sheila. "I'm, ah, I'm sorry, Sheila. I shouldn't have done that. Really, I'm not sure what came over me. I, I promise I won't do it again. It's just that ..."

Sheila put her finger on his lips and smiled at him. "It's okay, Ira. I liked it. And please promise me that you will do it again." Sheila stopped walking and looked into Ira's eyes. She moved her finger from his lips to his cheek. Slowly, a smile began to form.

"Can I ask you a question, my friend? I know this is probably a really stupid time to be asking questions, and I know I asked you a question the other night and you answered it, but I have another?"

"Ah, sure. What's on your mind?"

"I've been thinking about you. A lot." She tilted her head. "Tell me, why did you choose to become a rabbi? I think you could have done anything."

"I mean, really, Sheila." He pointed at Lloyd, who had stopped the four-wheeler. "We're being held hostage by a lunatic, we don't know if we'll escape or survive, and you want to know about my vocation?"

"Yes. I'm trying to think about positive things, and right now you're the only positive thought I have. So please. Humor me and please answer the question." Her smile grew. "And while you're at it, tell me why you dress the way you do."

Ira looked down at his clothes. "Okay. But we need to keep walking and, under the circumstances, I'll give you the *Readers Digest* version. I became a rabbi because, first and foremost, I'm Jewish. And I've always felt I had this special relationship with God. I believe in our Holy Scriptures, which consists of all the laws and traditions that Jewish people are supposed to follow. By the way, our Holy Scriptures is what you Christians call the Old Testament." Ira stole another glance at Lloyd. He had just lit a cigarette and appeared to be adjusting the load on the back of the four-wheeler. "I considered becoming a doctor—a cardiologist, mind you—and a lawyer. But in the end, becoming a rabbi seemed to be the best way to serve my community. So I began the studies and never looked back."

He doffed his hat, revealing his yarmulke. "As for how I dress, I only don this black suit for special purposes, or rites like the mezuzah ceremony I was going to perform for Irving and Fredda Moskowitz. Remember, I'm a liberal reformist Jew, not orthodox, and I believe that if I dress modestly people will see me and my personality, as it is, and not my clothes." He shrugged and smiled. "And that's it, in a nutshell." He rested his hand on her shoulder. "Satisfied?"

Sheila nodded.

Ira glanced over at Lloyd, who was staring at them. "It looks like our fearless leader is becoming anxious."

"Hey, you two assholes. If you're done playing touchy feely, get the hell over here." He chuckled. "There's a change of plans, and you're goin' to love it."

Ira and Sheila looked at each other, and their eyes spoke volumes. He put his arm around her again, and they walked over to Lloyd. Sheila put her hands on her hips and stared into the vacant space behind Lloyd's eyes. "What's the deal, Lloyd, are we stopping here for the night or did you call us to be in your presence for some other reason?"

"Always the smart ass, ain't you, Bitch."

Sheila refrained from responding. She could still feel the spots on her ankle and leg where he had kicked her, and her right cheek felt swollen and bruised where he had struck her.

"Like I said, there's a change of plans." He kicked the rear wheel of the ATV. "Gettin' too tough to drive this piece of shit. So here's the deal. We're walkin' and you two get to carry the little bit of grub we got left. And anything else you want." He held up the bag from the armored car. "Except for this. I'll take my ticket to a good life. Now let's head out while we still got some daylight."

Lloyd took two steps, stopped, and turned back to them with the .44 magnum in his hand. His sneer turned to a snarl. "Oh, and one more thing. Don't try nothin'." Waving the pistol he added, "Me and Mr. Ruger here will be watching you." He stared at them while returning the handgun to its reserved site between his jeans and belt. He raised his hand with his index finger extended and his thumb up and aimed at Sheila. He dropped his thumb and then blew over the end of his finger, mimicking blowing the smoke from a discharged weapon. A grin grew across his face as he winked at Sheila. He chuckled and began whistling while walking away.

Sheila placed her hand on her heart and let out a breath. "That man is certifiably, insanely scary."

Ira removed the bag containing their remaining provisions from the back of the ATV. He opened the bag. "There's only two potatoes left in here, and I don't think it makes any sense to carry them with us." He motioned throwing them aside, and when she nodded, he tossed them behind a log. He grabbed their blankets and Sheila's coat and shrugged. "Well, Sheila, we'd better follow him."

Sheila took her coat from Ira, momentarily rested her head on his shoulder, and took his hand. She smiled as she looked at him. "At least for a while."

CHAPTER 37

Brendan threw a couple of logs on the campfire, sat on the ground, and leaned against the log he had been sitting on. He put his arm around Susan, who nestled her head against his shoulder. He stared up at the cloudless star-filled sky and couldn't help but smile as he wondered if life could get any better than this. They'd had a great day. After setting up camp he'd caught some trout that he'd fried, along with some potatoes, for their supper. The kids were so tired they'd barely lasted long enough to enjoy the s'mores he'd made for dessert. He smiled again. *Nothing like s'mores made over a campfire.*

The tranquility of the evening was interrupted by the sound of brush breaking. Brendan sat up and turned his head toward the sound so he could hear better. There it was again. Another snapped twig. Straining to hear, he thought he heard someone talking. He removed his arm from Susan's shoulders and stood up. "Did you hear that, Susan? I thought I heard some branches break. We're supposed to be the only ones out here this weekend. What the hell . . ."

"Hey, in the camp! Okay to come in?"

Susan stood behind Brendan and held onto his arm. "Who's that, Brendan?"

"I have no clue. Some camper or hiker must be lost." He looked into the black of the night forest. "Yeah, it's okay. Come on in." He turned to Susan and shrugged. "What else could I say?"

It was like a scene from a macabre movie when the three people walked into the light of his campfire. The man in the lead, whose pocked face was topped with short greasy hair on top and a mullet hanging to his shoulders, was carrying some type of satchel. He was wearing black pants and a dirty white shirt and had a black stain on the right side of his neck. He was followed by a man wearing a black suit and a black hat. He had his arm around a disheveled middle-aged lady. Her blouse was torn, and her light brown shoulder-length hair looked like it had not seen a brush for days.

The leader walked closer. "Sorry to interrupt your night. Me and my friends here got lost. We had a four-wheeler, but the damn thing broke down. We kinda need a warm fire and some coffee to warm up a bit. And if you have any food to spare, well, we'd appreciate that too."

He walked up to the fire, and Brendan could now see that the stain was actually a tattoo of a spider. *Who the . . .?* But he caught himself. "Sure. Ah, come on in. We have some coffee left, don't we dear?"

"Yes. Ah, yes we do. And I think we have a few pieces of cold fish left as well."

"Well, that would be right nice because I am a bit hungry. My friends here ate a while ago, but I haven't for some time now. Seems that the little food we did have the dumb shits threw away." He pulled a pistol from his belt and then sat down on a log close to the fire.

"Jesus, what the hell . . . !" Brendan said.

"Oh, don't worry none." The man with the greasy mullet patted the handgun. "This is my friend Mr. Ruger. As long as everyone's cool, he'll be quiet. But I gotta tell ya that if things don't go my way, then he sometimes likes to talk. I gotta say, he's mighty loud when he talks and his bite stings." He shifted his gaze to Susan. "So there, Pretty Lady, how about that coffee and that fish now, huh?"

He pointed the pistol at his companions. "This here's a preacher man, and the broad's name is Sheila. I just call her

Bitch, though. Easier to remember." He stared at Susan until she moved behind her husband to be out of the intruder's sight.

He chuckled. "Hey, Preacher Man and Bitch," he called over his shoulder. "How about you come over here and join us. No sense in being lousy guests when people have invited us to their fire. These nice folks have some hot coffee for me and a bite of fish. Gonna save you from havin' to find somethin' to cook me tonight."

He pulled the hammer back on the handgun, pointed it at Sheila, and yelled, "Now!"

"Daddy, what's going on? Who are these people? And why does that man have a gun?" All heads turned to see Pete standing in his pajamas with his sister behind him. Vicki's arms hung straight at her sides, and she began to cry. Susan rushed to her children and knelt in front of them. She pulled them to her and put her arms around them.

She turned and stared at the intruder with a look that could have burned a hole through his chest. "What do you want and why are you here? These are just children, for God's sake! Take what you want and please leave us alone!"

"Mister, how about I give you some coffee in a thermos and the food we have and then you leave with your friends. We only want to have a fun family weekend camping before the children go back to school."

"Well, that's right friendly of you, I must say." The intruder's lips turned up in a sinister-looking smile. "I kinda like it here though. It's real comfortable. And warm." He pointed the .44 at Susan. "And I must say the scenery is right nice too. Yup, it's real pretty here." He turned his head so Brendan and Susan could see the tattoo, and his neck twitched, making the tarantula wiggle. "The more I think about it, the more I think we're goin' to stay here tonight."

He pointed the handgun at Susan. "Now how about you come over here and get me some of that coffee you said you had. And don't forget the fish."

Susan remained kneeling and pulled the children closer to her. She turned her back on this malevolent, gruesome creature that had breached their privacy and their lives. She buried her head in her son's chest and began to sob.

The intruder took the half-burned cigarette from his mouth and flicked it at the fire. "Jesus, not another one." He gazed at the ground and shook his head. "I've been dealing with this other bitch for days, and now I run into another one." He raised the handgun and cocked the hammer. "Like I said, Lady, if everybody does what I say, then Mr. Ruger here stays quiet. So . . ." He took a deep breath and exhaled slowly and audibly. "Now, dammit! I said now and I mean now! Do you hear me?"

Brendan jumped in front of the intruder and put his arms up. "Leave her alone! Don't you dare talk to my wife that way! You invade our campsite, and we've been trying to be nice. But now, you've crossed the line. Why don't you just get the hell out of here!" He motioned toward the woods. "And take your friends with you!"

Brendan never saw the pistol coming. It struck him on the left side of his face, knocking him to the ground. He thought his head had exploded. And now the ringing was like out-of-tune church bells. Before he could raise his hands, the intruder kicked him in the abdomen and Brendan thought his entire insides were going to come up. *What the hell is happening? Susan* . . . He tried to reach for the assailant's leg.

"You remind me of my former pissant partner." Lloyd kicked the outreached arm away and knelt on the gasping man's chest. He pushed the .44 magnum's muzzle into Brendan's forehead. "Do not, never, ever, talk to me like that! Got it, you stupid asshole?" His breathing became rapid as he pushed the pistol harder into Brendan's brow. He brought his face so close to Brendan's that their noses almost touched. Through clenched teeth he said, "You oughta know that I've killed assholes like you for a lot less."

He raised the pistol and fired into the ground beside Brendan's head. The sound echoed, fracturing the serenity of the evening.

Brendan heard Susan scream and tried to tell her he was okay, but he couldn't get the words out. The pain in his head and abdomen was so intense, and when he tried to catch his breath, it felt like there was a knife in his chest. *What the hell . . . Susan . . . Oh my God this hurts.*

Lloyd used the handgun to strike Brendan again in his right temple, ripping the skin open. Lloyd grinned as the adrenaline rushed through his system while he watched the blood streaming down the face of his victim. He grabbed Brendan's shirt at the neck and jerked his head up. His voice was a malicious half-whisper. "Now how 'bout you tell that pretty little wife of yours to get her pretty little ass over here and do like I told her to. Before you get hurt some more. You understand me, Asshole, cuz I promise you the next shot won't miss."

He pushed Brendan's limp body back to the ground and chuckled. "I guess you also oughta know that I like dessert after I eat supper and have my coffee." He glanced toward Susan. "And I think I know what I'm goin' to have."

He focused his gaze on Susan. "Listen, Lady. You better get over here right now before your man here really gets hurt. I'm gettin' hungrier and thirstier by the minute." His lip began to curl up and his neck twitched again, making the tarantula wiggle. "Like that, do you, huh? The babes all say it turns 'em on. You probably heard me tell your old man here about how I like dessert after I eat. Well, guess what?" He pointed the pistol at Susan. "I pick you." He turned to Sheila.

"Ah, I bet you feel bad, huh? You thought it was you tonight, didn't ya? Well, maybe I'll have seconds. Yeah, that's a great idea." He shrugged. "See. That's why everybody says I'm so smart."

"You sick, ugly bastard!" Susan was pointing at Lloyd while holding her children behind her with her other arm. "You heard me, you sick, ugly bastard! Get out of here! Now! And take your friends and that stupid-looking spider on your skinny little neck with you! And another thing, you asshole monster. Who the hell wears their hair like that anymore?" Her laugh was choked, but mocking. Her expression changed to one of pure rage and determination. "Now get the hell out of here!"

The intruder stood, paralyzed, for a moment. He slowly walked toward Susan until he was standing in front of her. He allowed a small grin to grow ever so slightly before his face changed to reflect the depravity of his soul. Susan stared into the most wicked pair of eyes she had ever encountered. They screamed evil and were boring through her. Susan's strength and composure began to ebb. She felt increasingly numb and defeated as the pent-up energy oozed from her body.

She never saw the backhand coming before it struck the side of her face. Her head snapped so hard she felt it had been propelled from her torso. She staggered back a foot before she regained her balance. She raised a hand to her face and felt the blood seeping from her open wound, wet and sticky.

Lloyd maintained his unblinking stare as he stepped toward Susan. He slapped both sides of her face, opening two more wounds. Susan's right eye began to swell shut. Lloyd grabbed the front of her blouse. He ripped it open, exposing her chest. His eyes dropped to her breasts and he smiled. "Nice." He nodded. "Them's real nice. I'm goin' to like them very much." He placed his hand on her shoulder, causing a shiver to course through her body. She could feel his poison, his evil. "Now how about, if you're calmed down, you get me that coffee and fish you promised." The smile grew. "Then we'll have dessert."

Lloyd had released his grip on her shoulder and was reaching for Susan's chest when he felt the sharp pain in his back, causing the air to escape in a loud whoosh. He fell forward and landed on Susan. He stood up and turned to see Ira standing with a small log in his hands. He pointed his pistol at the rabbi. "Well, Preacher Man. I never thought you'd have it in you. I must say, I am impressed." He shook his head. "But you never shoulda done that. You know that, don't ya?"

Ira threw the log toward the fire and raised his arms. "For all that is good and holy, please leave her alone," he pleaded. He gestured toward Peter and Vicki, who were kneeling by their injured, helpless father. "Please think about the children." He slowly lowered his arms. "These people haven't caused you or us any harm. Why don't we take the food they offered and leave?"

"You know, Preacher Man, you're lucky I like you. I certainly don't know why, and I can't for the life of me figure it out. But I do. Otherwise I woulda blown you away a long time ago." He pushed the weapon between his belt and jeans.

"Tell ya what we're goin' to do. I'm gonna have me a cup of that coffee Bitch Number Two over there promised me. And that fish. You see, I've kinda worked me up an appetite tonight. Then we're goin' to get these people all cozy for the night before Bitch Number One and I get outta here." He pointed at Sheila, who stood beside Brendan and the children. "I'm sure, being a smart man and all, you get the gist that I've decided the best thing for you is to stay with these people so I don't hurt you. Now ain't that nice of me?"

He shook his head and shrugged. "Just don't know why I'm givin' up a sure chance for my buddy Mr. Ruger to speak his piece, but it must be cuz I like you, Preacher Man. So it's time for you…" He pointed at Ira with his hand mimicking a pistol. "To count your blessings instead of tryin' to get 'em for other people."

Lloyd shifted his attention to Susan. "Okay, Lady. Just get me the coffee and the fish, and then me and the other bitch will be outta here. Okay?"

Susan had tucked her torn blouse around her. Not trusting this malevolent, barbaric, soulless man, she eased her way to the waning fire. Her right eye was swollen shut, but she maintained eye contact with her left eye as she slowly knelt. She put on an oven mitt and picked up the coffee pot. She filled a mug and set it down next to the fire. She retrieved the fish left over from their supper from the cooler and put them on a paper plate that she placed next to the coffee mug. She pointed at the food before skirting behind Ira, beside her husband and children.

Lloyd walked to the fire and picked up the coffee and fish. "See. Now that wasn't so hard, was it? If only you'd a done that right off the bat, things might've been different. But see, you're like most broads, my ma included. You just don't get it. You don't understand that men are the boss and you're supposed to do what we say." He stuffed a piece of fish in his mouth. When he began to speak again, some of the cold, batter-crusted trout flew out. "No questions asked."

"Lloyd, I've told you this before and I'm saying it again. You are one sick bastard."

Lloyd stopped chewing and, with food dribbling down his chin, stared at Sheila. It was the first time she had spoken since they arrived at the Brownlee campsite.

He pointed the coffee mug at her. "Now don't go gettin' me all riled up again. I just got settled down, and I'm tryin' to enjoy my supper before you and me head out into the night.

Hope you ain't scared of the boogie man, Bitch." He began to chuckle as he took another bite of the leftover trout.

When Lloyd had finished the fish and the coffee, he threw the dregs into the fire. He retrieved a cigarette from the flip-top box in his shirt pocket and lit it with a small burning twig he pulled from the fire. He took a long drag, blew the smoke out of his nose, and released a loud burp that caused him to chuckle. "Pretty cool, huh?" He pointed at Ira. "Okay, here's what we're goin' to do. Preacher Man, I want you to get me some rope from the tents." He looked at Peter. "Kid. You help the preacher man find what I want, okay? And find me a flashlight too. Now hurry up. We ain't got all night."

Peter grabbed the hand that Ira extended and led the rabbi toward the tent where his dad had stored their gear. They returned with a twenty-five foot length of clothesline rope and a flashlight, which Ira handed to Lloyd.

Lloyd flicked his wrist toward a large tree at the periphery of the campsite. "Okay, now I want all you over there by the tree. Sit down with your backs to the tree. Now!"

Ira and Sheila helped Brendan to his feet and helped him walk to the tree and sit down with his back against the trunk. Then the rest of them sat down.

"No, not you, Bitch." Lloyd pointed toward Sheila. "Didn't you hear me before? Me and you are leavin' together right after we make these people cozy. So you go put some wood on the fire and then stand there. And don't try nothin' stupid."

Lloyd had Ira hold an end of the rope as he walked around his captives. When he had finished securing the last knot, he stepped back and rubbed his hands together. "Now that should hold you for a while."

His gaze settled on Ira. He grabbed his hat and threw it into the fire. "It's not respectful to wear a hat, you know, in front of your superiors." He cocked his head and stared at Ira's yarmulke. "Well, look it here. Tell me, just why are you wearin' that stockin' cap? It's not winter yet. Some things about you, Preacher Man, I just plain don't get."

Lloyd stood in front of Brendan. Susan pulled her husband as close to her as her bindings would allow.

"You know, this coulda been a lot easier if you just wouldn't have pissed me off," Lloyd said. He took another long drag on his Marlboro and blew the smoke at Susan and Brendan. "So, I think it only right that I leave you a little reminder of me. Maybe next time you won't be so sassy when someone's givin' you orders." He squatted in front of Brendan, took another drag from the shrinking cigarette, and blew the smoke at him. He took the glowing butt from his mouth and extinguished it on Brendan's exposed forearm, causing him to shriek in pain.

Susan screamed and strained at the rope holding her to the tree. "You animal! You piece of shit! Why'd you do that? Haven't you caused him and us enough pain?"

Lloyd just smiled as he picked up the flashlight and walked over to the fire. He reached out his hand toward Sheila. "Okay. It's time for me and you to get goin'. I guess we're not wanted here any longer."

Sheila looked at his hand and then straight into Lloyd's eyes before spitting in his face.

Lloyd grabbed her arm and began pulling her toward the night. "I just wish you wouldn't always do such dumb, stupid things. Guess that's why you're a bitch, huh?"

CHAPTER 38

Benno knelt by the stream, cupped his hands, and scooped some of the cold water and poured it over his head. The water dripped from his face and hair back to the stream, creating small circles that coalesced and became one with the stream again. He scooped more of the frigid water and held it against his closed, swollen right eye. The burn on his forearm hurt like hell, and Benno couldn't tell if it was red from the trauma or if it was beginning to become infected. The water felt like ice, but was also soothing and medicinal. He repeated the process for about half an hour, cleansing his wounds and pressing the gelid liquid against his eye until his teeth chattered and his body shivered uncontrollably from the cold. But he thought the swelling had decreased, offering a small slit through which he could see with his right eye.

His headache had lessened and the pain from the burn had become tolerable, but the pain in his groin . . . God his balls hurt. *You son of a bitch, Lloyd. I'm gonna pay you back good.* He considered sitting in the water to see if it would help, but thought he should warm up first. He ambled to the fire and discovered a few embers were still glowing. It didn't take much to tease them back to life and, within minutes, he was sitting before a roaring fire, the heat seeking out every crevice in his body and driving out the cold.

When the shivering ceased, he attempted to walk. He only made it three steps before the pain intensified, causing him to bend over. He gently touched his scrotum. *God, it feels like I've got nuts the size of balloons. Or of an elephant.* He shook his head. *I ain't got no choice. I gotta sit in that damn cold water and see if I can shrink 'em down some.*

He threw a couple of logs on the fire and slowly walked to the stream with his legs spread like he had just dismounted from riding a horse all day. Benno walked into the stream still holding his scrotum. *This is gonna hurt.*

He eased himself into a sitting position, and the cold consumed him. Still clutching himself, he screamed, "Son of a bitch, this hurts!" He persevered until he thought he would bounce on the stream's bottom because of the shivering. He left the stream and shuffled to the fire's edge. It took three freeze-and-thaw sessions before the scrotal pain and swelling diminished to a level of tolerability.

He threw dead pine logs on the fire until it was again blazing and then lay down as close as possible without singeing his hair or burning his clothes. The crackling of the dry pine logs as they were being devoured by the fire was calming, and the heat eased the tension in his muscles allowing him to relax. His thoughts turned to revenge. A plan was beginning to form when he heard the shot. Startled, he sat up, causing the headache to escalate. He grabbed his head. "Dammit!"

Benno rocked back and forth until the pain subsided. He gazed in the direction of the sound. *I wonder what that dumb son of a bitch did now.*

Surrendering to exhaustion he eased himself to the ground. He picked up the .38 Ruger handgun and laid it on a small log next to him. He tried to smile. *You're goin' to be sorry you left this little baby, Lloyd.* His last thought before allowing the inevitable sleep to overcome him was, *I'll find him tomorrow. Then I'll get even.* A smile began to form as his eyelids drooped and his breathing became heavy.

CHAPTER 39

The brilliance of the rising moon enabled Roberto to find his way to the top of the ridge without difficulty. Using his night-vision binoculars, he scanned the horizon but didn't see any evidence of Malin or Donnrud and their hostages. He sat on a log with his head in his hands and thought about Clyde. He couldn't imagine who would want to hurt an old man like Clyde. Roberto could picture Clyde standing at the door whenever he arrived for a visit. He would be clad in his faded blue jeans and patched red and black flannel shirt with his thinning gray hair neatly combed. And he would inevitably be holding his Bible. The more he thought about it, the angrier he became, and his resolve to find the perpetrators heightened.

Then his thoughts turned to Jesse. His life had been pretty simple until she appeared at the hat box. He sensed he was changing. He was softening and a part of him he had forgotten existed was resurfacing. He was sure he hadn't smiled as much in the past twenty years as he had in the last few days. He welcomed the change, but was unsure of how to deal with the fear of the future. The pain from the last time, the only time, he had totally given himself to another was still palpable. He kicked at the ground. *Damn that Lori Lynn.*

But he had to admit that Jesse was different. She wasn't demanding. His impression was that she just wanted to be an equal and for their relationship to be built upon a strong friendship. Roberto picked up a rock and threw it into the night. *Yeah, she's okay. I think I could like this girl and this could work. When this is over I'm going to give it a shot and see what happens.*

Bogey, who had been lying by his side, rose and his body stiffened. A low growl began to form deep in his chest. Roberto knew from experience that his friend and bodyguard sensed danger. Roberto began scratching Bogey's ears. "What is it, Boy? You smell that old griz out there? Maybe we'd better head back down to camp."

He had taken a few steps to begin the descent when the calm of the night was cleaved by the echoing sound of a gunshot. Roberto instinctively fell to the ground with momentary flashbacks to a night patrol in Nam. The sound echoed across the mountaintops and gradually faded. As the quiet of the mountain night resumed its omnipresence, Roberto stood and gazed in the direction of the shot. *So that's where you are? I knew you'd screw up sooner or later and tell me where you were.* He pointed his finger. "Gotcha."

Roberto looked at the campfires below. Nube and Jess would already be asleep. He leaned down and petted his friend. "Let's go, Pal. Tomorrow's going to be a good but long day."

When he arrived at their campsite, he could hear the deep breathing of Nube and Jesse and knew they were sound asleep. They had done a decent job of banking the perimeter fires, but they would require more wood if they were going to burn through the night and, hopefully, keep that stalking grizzly away.

After he had stoked all the fires, including their cooking fire, Roberto placed his Colt 1911a1 handgun on a log and leaned his Herstal .338 Magnum against the same piece of dried, decaying wood. He unrolled his sleeping bag next to the log, but chose to lie on top rather than undress and climb in. He knew he needed to rest, but a sixth sense told him he could not allow himself to fall into a deep slumber. Not with that bear out there. And he wanted to get an early start now that he had an idea where the perps were.

Before closing his eyes he glanced at Jesse to make sure she was in her sleeping bag and it was zipped closed. A smile formed on his face as his eyes became heavy.

CHAPTER 40

Roberto knew he was only partially awake, but he also knew that he was dreaming—again. He felt that a prohibitive force would not allow him to fully awaken. Nor would it allow him to succumb to the open arms of deep slumber. He was walking through the charred remnants of yesterday's lush, green jungle, now reduced to various shades of gray. The once verdant floor now blanketed with shredded foliage beneath splintered trees with their branches hanging like half-mast flags, strewn with the individual bodies of soldiers who had been writhing with the agony of their wounds. But now, lying in the stillness of their deaths, they all looked alike. The air was filled with the humming of a continuous note as smoke emanated from their mouths.

There it was again, the pleading of a dying comrade, one of his soldiers, calling for a medic. And the sobbing of the medic who somehow, by the grace of God, like his leader, had survived this massacre, "I'm so sorry, Sarge. I'm so sorry. I failed again."

ROBERTO'S THRASHING AROUND AND MOANING awakened Jesse. She was beginning to crawl out of her sleeping bag when he yelled, "Medic! Where the hell are you? Stop your damn crying and help these guys!"

Jesse crawled over to him and gently shook his shoulder. "Rob. Rob. Wake up. It's okay, Rob. I'm here."

He had rolled onto his left side, and when she touched his shoulder, he swung his right arm around and knocked her over. "Jeez, Rob."

The sound of Jesse's voice awakened him. "Jess, what the hell . . . I'm sorry. Ah shit, did I hurt you? Oh, God, Jess, I'm sorry. Are you okay?"

Rubbing her lip, she said, "Yeah, I'm okay. What was going on? You were moaning and thrashing around. And then you started yelling about a medic."

Roberto sat up and touched Jesse's face. "Did I hit you in the face? Oh, God, Jess, I'm so sorry."

"I'm okay, Rob. Honest. Now tell me what was going on."

He gazed at the ground, took a deep breath, and rubbed his temples. When he looked up at Jesse, she thought he had the saddest and most distant but most honest expression she had seen on him. He reached over and took her hand in his. "Remember that ride in the truck, from Billings to my place, when I told you that I was having recurrent nightmares and that I was not ready to talk to you about them?"

Jesse just nodded and squeezed his hand.

A faint, momentary smile appeared on Rob's face before he resumed a serious countenance. "Well, it's time. My last mission was just plain horrible, Jess. I lost all my men, the whole squad, except the medic. Stuart Lipscomb was his name." He paused a moment. "I lost track of him over the years, and for a while I couldn't even remember his name. I wouldn't be surprised if he committed suicide. He just couldn't deal with the fact that all those young kids died and he couldn't save them. It didn't matter how bad they were shot up or how many times I told him it wasn't his fault. I was the leader of that patrol, Jess. Not him. It was my fault all those kids died. Remember when I gave you those statistics and especially the one about the more than 33,000 eighteen-year-olds who were killed?" When she nodded he dropped her hand and jabbed his right thumb into his chest. "That was my squad, a bunch of eighteen-year-olds. Most didn't even shave yet. I was in charge and should have been able to do something that would have prevented that massacre. They were just kids, Jess."

He picked up a small stick and threw it at the fire. "All these years, all the hours of therapy, and I still have the nightmares. I still see their faces and hear the kids yelling for me. And I hear that poor dumb-shit medic crying and telling me he's sorry." His voice rose. "He's sorry? What about me?" He put his hands on his ears, dropped his head, and let the pent-up tears begin to flow down his dust-covered face.

Jesse allowed him a moment before crawling into the space between his arms. She reached up and wiped a small rivulet of tears from his face. "Let it go, Rob. Let it go and let it be."

The tears clouded his eyes and began to flow down his face like small rivers after a springtime thaw. His chest heaved and he started to sob. "Oh, Jess, you don't know how I'd like to do that, but you gotta understand, I can't un-see what I've seen. I just can't."

He dropped his arms, pulled her to him, and held her tight. He continued to sob for a few minutes and then wiped the tears from his face with the backs of his sleeves. He pulled Jesse to him again and nestled his face into her hair and then laid his head on hers. He reached up and touched her face and began to slowly draw his thumb across her cheek.

After allowing some time to compose himself, he whispered to her, "I remember one of my first counselors, some guy I talked to before getting out of the Army. He told me about Joshua Lawrence Chamberlain. Ever hear of him?"

She shook her head.

"He was a colonel in the 20th Maine regiment in the Civil War and was awarded the Medal of Honor for his service at Gettysburg. Anyway, my counselor told me Colonel Chamberlain once said that wars are fought by young men who have nothing to say about where they are being sent to die. Man, that hit me right between the eyes and should have been enough to ease my pain. I think of those words quite often, sometimes daily. But it's not enough, Jess. I can't get beyond the feeling that I failed all those young kids. In so many ways I feel like I killed them."

"Oh, Rob. That speaks to your compassion, and it's what made you the great leader you were and the great man that you are." She looked into his eyes. "You're a good man, Rob. Trust me on that. Lord knows I've encountered more than my share of duds." She stroked his cheek. "You see yourself as just a man with an imperfect past. But you're a good man now, and that's what counts." She leaned up and kissed him, and he found himself returning the kiss.

He pulled away and put his hand on the back of her head. "Thanks Jess. I think you just did more than all the damn psych-guys I've seen over the years combined. Now we better get some rest. Tomorrow is going to come sooner than we think, and it's going to be a hard day. I heard a shot when I was up on the ridge, and I think I know about where those assholes are at."

"Okay, but I'm sleeping right here with you." With a hint of a coy smile, she added, "and this time there's no sending me to my own room."

Jesse stood up and retrieved her sleeping bag. She lay down next to Rob and pulled her bag over them. He was holding her and thinking about what she had said and was starting to feel good about himself for the first time in years.

"Rob, you still awake?"

"Yeah, why?"

"I think I'm beginning to fall in love with you, Rob. Now get some sleep." She smiled as she snuggled in closer to him. She closed her eyes and wondered about the expression on his face.

Roberto smiled and remembered reading that the voice is more than half the love.

CHAPTER 41

The first streaks of gray were replacing the ebony of night when Roberto was awakened by Bogey's low growl. He glanced at the fires. They had burned down to glowing embers. *Damn, how could I allow myself to fall asleep?* He eased himself away from Jesse and placed his hand on Bogey's back. Roberto felt the dog's taut muscles and knew that all hell was about to break loose.

"Easy boy." His whispered breath condensed in the cool autumn morning. He grabbed his Colt, but before he could strap on the holster, the solitude of the early morning was ruptured by the ground-shaking roar of the old grizzly. Jesse's piercing scream drowned out the "What the hell . . .?" that Nube managed before Bogey growled and lurched toward the clamor of the oncoming intruder.

"Bogey!" Roberto scrambled to his feet, but before he could follow his friend, he heard the large canine yelp and then whine.

"You son of a bitch . . ." Roberto fired his handgun at the shadow of the roaring predator. Undaunted, the bear came into camp, stood his full seven feet, and roared again. Roberto kept walking toward him, firing his handgun until the clip was empty. He continued to pull the trigger and walk toward this immense invader, but the giant omnivore was not fazed. He dropped to all fours, turned his head, and roared again. He took two steps toward Roberto, and it appeared they could easily reach out and touch each other. The griz stood on his hind feet again and swatted at the ducking Roberto. The glancing blow from the razor-sharp three-inch claws tore his shirt and the skin of his left shoulder, leaving his arm feeling numb.

The deafening three-round burst from Nube's Colt M4 rifle with its NATO 5.56 x 45 mm ammunition traveled just past Roberto's left ear and struck the immense trespasser in the chest with a thud. The combined effect of the grizzly's swat and the concussive blast from Nube's rifle knocked Roberto to the ground. He had enough time to roll to his side before the grizzly collapsed next to him.

Nube ran over and approached the unmoving creature from behind. He placed the muzzle of his rifle against the back of the bear's skull and nudged him. Although there was no response, he fired a single shot into its calvarium. Assured the animal was now dead, he looked at Roberto, who had risen to his knees and was holding his left shoulder. Jesse was kneeling by his side, caressing his face and trying to remove his hand from his shoulder so she could examine his wounds. Without moving his rifle, Nube asked, "You okay, Rob?"

When he didn't respond, Nube asked again, in a louder voice, "Rob, you okay?"

Roberto began rocking back and forth while shaking his head. He released the grip on his shoulder and placed a finger in his ear. He slowly stood and looked at Nube. "That shot was damn close to my head." He continued to shake his head and dig in his ear with his finger. "I think you might have ruptured my eardrum."

"Would you hold still, Rob, so I can check your shoulder."

"Don't worry about me." He removed Jesse's hand from his shoulder and looked around. "Where's my dog? Bogey! Where are you, Boy?"

They heard a low whimper and saw the bullmastiff limp into the light of the dying campfire. Roberto knelt and Bogey limped over to him. A cursory glance assured Roberto that his friend's wounds were superficial, but they would need attention. He put his right arm around Bogey's head and cradled him to his chest. Bogey looked up and slobbered a comforting lick on Roberto's face.

Jesse knelt and put her arms around both of her men. Bogey dutifully licked away the tears streaming down her face.

"If you three are finished with your heart-tugging, Hallmark moment, how about you move to the fire so we can examine and clean your wounds?"

Jesse looked up at the smiling Nube, who was still prodding the back of the deceased grizzly's head with the muzzle of his rifle.

"He's right, Rob. Come on, let's get you and Bogey over here where we can clean you up."

Roberto sat on a log, cradling his left arm by his side, and Bogey lay at his feet. He reached down and stroked Bogey's head. He glanced skyward to give thanks that he and his best friend had survived the grizzly's attack and noted the orange shards of dawn piercing the early morning gray. Nube retrieved their first aid kit while Jesse began boiling some water over the stoked fire. It took Nube and Jesse about fifteen minutes to clean and dress the wounds. By the time they had completed their care, Roberto had regained the sensation in his arm and was able to put the limb through a painful range of motion. He picked up a stick and was satisfied that his grip had also returned. He shook his head again, and after digging his finger in his ear, he looked at Nube with a grin. "Thank God my hearing is back. Otherwise I might have had to poke a sharp stick in your ear while you were sleeping just to get even."

"Is that the thanks I get for saving your life?" Nube said.

Jesse put her hands on her hips. "Okay, you two, knock it off. No fighting." She looked at Nube. "How about you help me prepare some breakfast. I'm sure our fearless leader is itching to get started this morning."

"If you don't mind, Jess, I think I'd better call in and check with my boss again. Agent Benson gave me strict orders last night to call him and if I don't. . . well, let's just say that I sure don't want the adage of my ass being grass and him being a lawn mower to be played out."

Nube returned to the fire after completing his morning update with Special Agent in Charge Benson. He closed his eyes, tilted his head back, and inhaled the savory aroma of freshly brewing coffee and frying bacon.

"Jess, that smells so good you just might bring that old griz back to life. Speaking of that critter, have you guys ever seen anything so ugly?" He chuckled. "Reminds me of the deputy I worked with in Minnesota, Pete Mohr. He had a couple of sayings he liked to use for less–than-attractive people or animals. He either said they were as ugly as death eating a soda cracker or they were not a front-porch geranium."

Roberto shook his head. "Enough with the nonsensical bullshit, Nube. What'd your boss say about Clyde?"

Nube squatted by the fire and filled a mug with the steaming coffee. After taking a small sip he exclaimed its delectability with a prolonged, "Ahhhhhhh."

"Agent Benson said your friend Clyde is better. He's not out of the woods, but the docs say he's improved and he should be able to be discharged from the ICU in a couple of days. He also informed me of something that you're not going to like. It's his impression that we should've found the perps and their hostages by now, so he's sending up a recon bird. As you both know, our office works closely with Carbon and Yellowstone Counties on search and rescue missions, and Benson has asked Fly Bird to put up one of their SAR choppers to see if they can spot 'em."

Roberto leaped to his feet and winced as he attempted to lift his left arm. "Jesus, Nube! I specifically said when we met in Chief Brennan's office that I thought stealth was the best option. If those two assholes kill those two innocent hostages, there will be hell to pay. Mark my words—their blood will not be on my hands. I'd suggest you call your boss again and tell him, in no uncertain terms, that I said he should shove that idea up his bureaucratic ass. And another thing. .."

He cocked his head to the side and half closed his eyes. "Shit! Forget it. I hear the bird." He looked at the sky. "My guess is Fly Bird's using their Sikorsky." He paused. "That chopper's equipped with thermal imaging gear. They should be able to detect a warm body with that equipment, even in a forest as dense as this one." He followed the sound of the chopper as it made its way across the mountaintop to their west. "I guess the positive is that they may help us locate 'em before the assholes go postal."

He threw the remains of his still-steaming coffee into the ebbing fire. "I suggest we get moving. The perps will also hear the bird, and we may not have much time to find the hostages… Alive."

CHAPTER 42

Benno was still curled up next to the dying fire when the three-shot salvo from Nube's M4 rifle shattered the quiescence of the early morning. He jumped up causing an escalation of his subsiding pain. The right side of his face immediately began throbbing, and he squeezed his swollen scrotum between his thighs, triggering a searing pain and leaving him momentarily breathless.

"Holy shit! What the hell was that?" As the throbbing ebbed he looked up, rocking back and forth, still holding his head and scrotum.

"What the . . . who the hell is that?" He struggled to his feet. "Well, whoever the hell it is, they're close. So Benno, you better get your sweet ass movin'."

One step told him it would be a while before he'd be able to walk with any speed or comfort. He closed his left eye. Despite the swelling, he could see with his right eye. He should try to put some cold water on his wounds again. When he began walking to the stream, his pants felt heavy and still damp from the repeated soakings the previous day.

Well I gotta clean my eye and my arm, but I ain't sittin' in that shit today. I'll never be able to walk if I do.

He was pouring the frigid water over his head when he heard the helicopter. The water dripped from his head and hands as he looked up trying to locate this second intrusion into an already wretched morning. Instinctively he began to curl up into as small a ball as his tortured body would allow. It only took a few seconds for him to realize what was happening. "Shit. Now they've got helicopters huntin' us. Time to move."

He walked back to the log where he had placed the pistol. Bending over to pick it up caused another surge of pain in his head. He spun the cylinder of the .38 Ruger revolver and noted there were two live rounds. He chuckled as he flipped his wrist to secure the cylinder. "Thanks for leavin' me two rounds, Asshole. You get both of 'em, you lousy piece of shit."

He could still hear the search and rescue chopper in the distance as he shoved the pistol into the right front pocket of his pants and began to slowly follow the ATV tracks.

CHAPTER 43

Ira had spent a restless, fitful, cold night. Brendan's intermittent moaning and Susan's attempts to quiet and reassure him, as well as the children's occasional sobs, were bad enough. But to sit on the hard ground, without a blanket, with his back against a tree and a rope wound around his chest three times . . . well, it was impossible to sleep.

Ira stared at what was left of their fire. Only a few logs still had a dull red hue. He didn't think there was enough heat to warm up a single cup of coffee, to say nothing of five people. He was beginning to shiver, and the children were complaining to their mother about the cold. He had been able to free his hands behind him and had spent the last hour attempting to pull the rope around him so he could untie the knot. He recalled how Lloyd had snickered when he placed the knot between Brendan and Vickie, knowing neither would be able to untie it. Ira could only guess at the severity of Brendan's wounds. He had to free them all and warm them up, or there would be the potential problem of shock and hypothermia.

Three shots shook the dark from the night and startled them all except for Brendan, who seemed incapable of responding. The children began to cry despite Susan's comforting words.

"Ira, what in the world was that?"

"I'm not sure, but whoever fired those shots is not that far away. How's your husband?"

He could tell she was struggling to maintain her composure. "I'm scared, Ira. He won't respond to me."

"Can you check his pulse? Do you know how?"

"Yes, yes I do. I. . . I think I can feel it in his neck, but it's pretty weak. And fast."

"We need to get him warmed up. I need your help, Susan. I, we, need you to stay strong. I'm trying to pull the rope around so I can untie the knot. I want you to help me, okay?"

"Sure. I'll try. Which of the three ropes do I pull?"

"Let's do the middle one. Pull to your left on the count of three, okay?"

A single shot rang out and was amplified as it echoed across the mountain lake. It drained the last semblance of composure from Susan, and she began sobbing uncontrollably, causing her children to cry.

Between gasps and sobs Vickie said, "Mommy, what's happening to us?"

Peter screamed, "I don't want to die!"

"Susan! Susan! Listen to me! You've got to get control of yourself and the children if we're going to get out of this."

Susan's chest-heaving cries began to diminish. "I'm sorry, Ira. But I'm scared. Scared out of my mind."

"I know you are. But we have to try to stay calm so we can get out of this mess."

Ira could hear her whispering to her children. The gentleness of her voice even reassured him. "Okay, Ira. I, ah, I think we're okay now. At least I think we can help you with this rope."

After repeated efforts the rope would not budge. Finally Susan said, "Ira, I think that animal tied the rope around Brendan's waist. I can feel a knot, but I can't get it loose and I can't move it."

Ira's head had dropped in defeat when he heard the first sounds of the rescue chopper. "Shh, Susan. Listen." He turned his head to the repeated "whup, whup, whup" of rotor blades. "You hear that, Susan! That's a helicopter! I'd bet it's a search and rescue team. It won't be long now, Susan, and someone will be here to rescue us. Let's just stay calm and give thanks to God."

CHAPTER 44

The orange slivers of dawn were piercing the early morning gray when Sheila awoke. She thought it was the shivering that had awakened her, but it was also being very uncomfortable. Lloyd had allowed her to keep her coat but taken her blanket. He had tied her hands behind her back and secured the rope to a small deciduous tree. The fire he had built had burned down to a few glowing embers. She grinned as she thought how inept and simple Lloyd was. But the grin faded as she quickly reminded herself just how frighteningly dangerous he also was. He couldn't build a fire to last a night, but he'd just as soon kill you as look at you. She would have to ask Ira how God, who creates all things good and beautiful, could also create something so despicable. Or why He would want to.

She was pondering that question while listening to the morning's breeze rustling through the leaves. She glanced up and watched as an unyielding victim was pried loose and floated to its final resting place on the forest's floor. The irony of the moment was not lost on her, and a single tear began making its way down her cheek.

Sheila was startled back to reality by the three-round burst of a rifle. Her head jerked to the north. *Who?* But it only took a moment for her to realize that they were not out here alone. She looked at Lloyd who had sat up and thrown his blanket aside.

"What the hell was that?" Lloyd picked up the .44 magnum and rose to a crouch. "Where the hell did that come from? Huh? You hear that shot, Bitch?"

Sheila eased herself to a standing position, smiling at Lloyd, who appeared bewildered and frightened. "They're coming, Lloyd. And you can't stop 'em. So what are you going to do now, Big Man?"

Lloyd was looking frantically in all directions when they heard the fourth shot. He twisted toward the sound of the echo and fired the Ruger. The bullet passed through the tree above Sheila's head. She screamed and dropped to the ground, trying to bury her head in her coat.

Lloyd remained crouched, and his eyes widened as he assumed the two-handed hold on the pistol grip. He kept swinging the handgun back and forth while searching through the dense trees for whoever had fired a rifle.

"Come out you sons-a-bitches! You ain't takin' me alive! And if you shoot one more time, I'm shootin' the bitch here! Got it?"

A few minutes later, he slowly stood and walked over to Sheila. She was crying and her head was still buried in the shoulder of her coat. Lloyd kicked her in the shin. "Shut up! You hear me? Get your ass up. We're gettin' outta here." She didn't move so he kicked her again. "I said now and I mean now! We're gettin' the hell outta here right goddamn now!"

Sheila stood and glared at her captor. "Would you at least untie my hands so I can go to the bathroom? And I might be able to walk easier and faster if my hands are free. Or are you afraid that I might run away?"

Lloyd returned the stare before tucking his pistol in the small of his back. He shook his head. Then he turned so she could see him bring his tarantula to life in his twitching neck. He snickered. "For a broad, I gotta say you got your-self one set of balls. More than that stupid ass Benno. Turn around so I can untie you." Before she could turn, however, he grabbed her shoulder. "But I'm takin' the rope with me, just in case I need it to tie you up again." He shrugged and his neck twitched again. "Never can tell, Bitch."

CHAPTER 45

Nube squatted and picked up a crumpled cigarette butt. He shook the dirt free and turned it around in his hand. He held it up and looked at Roberto, who was kicking the tire of the abandoned ATV. "Hey, Rob. I found another cigarette butt. It's a Marlboro just like all those we found at the camp-site back about half a click. One of those guys sure smokes a lot." He flicked the butt to the side and walked over to where Roberto was inspecting the ATV. "Is this your friend Clyde's machine?"

"Yeah, this is his four-wheeler. It doesn't look too much worse for wear."

Jesse joined her companions and held up a small bag. She nodded to her left. "I found this behind a log over there. It looks like they decided not to keep a couple of potatoes. Either they stuffed some food in their pockets, or they're soon going to be getting very hungry." She tossed the bag to the side of the trail and rested her hand on Roberto's arm. "Any thoughts on what's happening?"

"I'm not sure." He looked at Nube. "You have any thoughts, Mr. FBI?"

Nube removed his ball cap with the bright gold FBI letters embroidered across the front. He scratched his head before resetting his cap. "Based upon what we found at the other site, two .38 casings, live embers in the fire, the ground disturbed like there had been a struggle, and the dirt still wet in places, my guess is that the two perps had a falling out, they fought, and one was left behind, presumably injured and probably shot. And I'd have to guess that it was Malin who injured Donnrud. But it would appear that Donnrud, if indeed he was the victim, was able to recover enough to pursue Malin and the two hostages."

Nube kicked at the dirt as he stared off in the direction he assumed the perpetrators were heading. He squatted, picked up some dirt, and let it run through his fingers. "One more thing, I'd also have to guess that the last one to pass here is only a half hour ahead of us." He threw the last of the dirt he was holding aside. "At most."

Before Roberto could respond, they heard the helicopter coming close on another pass. Nube's Iridium 9555 sat phone began to ring at the same time. "This is Agent Lawson."

"This is Charlie Brayer in Fly Bird niner-one-one-two-one. We've been asked by FBI Special Agent in Charge Benson to assist in your pursuit and apprehension of two felons and the rescue of their two hostages. He told me to call you, and he also told me Roberto DeLaCroix is with you. Is that affirmative?"

Nube glanced at Roberto. "That's affirmative."

"May I speak with him please? He and I go way back on search and rescue missions."

Nube handed the phone to Roberto. "He wants to talk to you."

Roberto glanced to the south and attempted to spot the chopper. "This is Roberto DeLaCroix."

"Hey, Rob. Charlie Brayer here. Tell me where you're at."

He smiled and nodded in recognition of his friend's voice. "Remember the elbow in Whiskey River, where I told you I found an old whiskey bottle on my first trout guide and where you caught the twenty-four inch rainbow? That's where we're at."

Within moments Charlie had the cardinal red and brilliant white Sikorsky hovering about fifty yards east of them. Rob pointed south along the serpentine path of the mountain stream. He yelled into the sat phone, "They're following the river."

"Keep your phone open. We'll let you know what we find." The veteran pilot banked the SAR chopper and began moving downstream. Rob heard a blip on the phone and then Charlie's voice. "You've got a single about two clicks south about to enter a campsite on the northeast side of Wild Bill Lake. Appears to be others in the campsite."

"Can you tell how many?"

"That's a negative. We'll take a look from another angle. Hang on."

Roberto could hear the continuous thumping of the Sikorsky's rotors. "We've got a visual on two more, about two clicks west of Wild Bill. I'm not sure where they're headed. Troy, one of my volunteers, just told me . . . Jesus, Rob, they just shot at us! We're out of here!"

Roberto flinched at the sound of the .44. Even at this distance the bark of the Ruger was ear-rending. "Get the hell out of there, Charlie! Go to the campsite. We'll catch up."

Roberto handed the sat phone to Nube and pulled on his backpack. "Let's go. One of them, I'm guessing Malin, just shot at Charlie's chopper. He's about three clicks southwest of here. He doesn't know where he's going. But I do. They're headed for Devil's Gorge."

CHAPTER 46

Benno had discovered the abandoned ATV and continued following Lloyd's trail. He smiled whenever he came across a scuff mark in the ground or a broken twig. It was his guess that Sheila was doing her part to assist whoever would be pursuing them.

The sound of crying had led him to the edge of the woods. He stayed in the shadows and gazed at a campsite on the shore of a glass-like lake. He could see a lady, two children, and what appeared to be a man crumpled over on the lady, tied to a large tree. He was about to enter the clearing when he heard the helicopter again. Then he heard a voice he recognized. *The preacher man's here. Must be tied up on the other side of that tree.*

Benno walked into camp as quickly as his painful, swollen scrotum would allow. He stayed in the shadows, and what he saw caused a wave of nausea to surge through him, and he thought he was steeled to the sights, sounds and smells of violence. The lady's hair was disheveled, her face was bruised, swollen, and dirty, her blouse had been torn, and her shoes were off. The two kids were crying and shivering. And the man . . . holy shit. He looked like he'd had the shit kicked out of him. His shirt was torn and there were numerous cuts on his face. One eye was swollen shut, his left hand was swollen, and he had an open wound with crusted blood on his forearm. The ropes were prohibiting the lady's attempts to aid him.

Benno moved out of the shadows, and when the lady saw him, she yelled, "Ira, there's another one of them!"

Benno turned his back on them and walked to the fire. He squatted and picked up some of the firewood stacked next to their fire pit. He poked at the dying embers with a small, dry twig until the fire came to life. He threw on a couple of logs and then poured some water from a pail next to the fire ring into a pot hanging over the fire.

"Benno, I'm glad to see you're okay," Ira said. "Susan, the lady here, put a knife in the cooler next to the fire. Would you please get it and cut us loose?"

"Which way did the asshole go, Preacher Man?"

"Please," Susan said. "Please cut us loose. I need to help my husband."

"Which way, Preacher Man?"

Ira nodded toward the southwest. "Lloyd took Sheila and headed that way."

Benno walked in the direction Ira had indicated, and he heard another gunshot. He stopped and stared toward the origin of the sound, which was still echoing throughout the clearing. He shook his head, pulled out the .38, and spun the cylinder. He nodded when he saw that the two rounds were still in place.

Benno turned around and looked at Ira and the other four. He walked over to the cooler and retrieved the knife. He looked at Ira and shrugged. "Oh what the hell." He squatted next to Ira and cut the ropes, freeing the hostages from their bondage. "I guess I owed you that, Preacher Man. For what you and Sheila did for me." Still holding the knife, he stood and began flicking his wrist. "You help these folks, Preacher Man. I'm goin' after that sumbitch Lloyd."

He heard the chopper coming close. "Take care, Preacher Man. I'll try to help your lady friend." He threw the knife, and it stuck into the ground next to Ira's feet. And then he turned and walked into the woods.

CHAPTER 47

Lloyd heard the helicopter veering toward them. The tops of the trees began to bend from the downdraft of the rotors. The yellowing leaves loosened from their death grip and being strewn about was lost on this malevolent creature as he attempted to locate the SAR chopper. He released his grip on Sheila's arm, grabbed her hair, and pushed her to the ground. He spotted the chopper as it banked just at the edge of a clearing. Lloyd could see someone hanging out the side door, and he instinctively fired the .44 while holding it with one hand, Dirty Harry style. The twelve-pound recoil proved excessive for even someone as gun-savvy as Lloyd, and he fired wide of the hovering search vehicle.

Lloyd snickered as he pointed the handgun at the helicopter, which had accelerated and banked as it retreated. As he watched the withdrawing chopper, his snicker escalated into an insanely grotesque snort.

"You sons-a-bitches ain't takin' me alive! Hear me? Not the bitch here, either!"

He looked down at Sheila who had rolled herself into as small a target as she could. Lloyd released the cylinder and spun it around. "Two left. One for them and one for you." He pointed the Ruger at her., "You just didn't get it did ya? It coulda been good between us. I thought all along that I'd get rid of that pissant Benno and that you and me would share this loot. We coulda had a good life you and me." He shook his head. "But no. You had to be so goddamn snippy and bitchy all the time. I just don't get you broads. You just don't know your place, and you don't know when you got a good thing." He looked down and kicked at an invisible stone.

When he returned his gaze to Sheila she noted his appearance and demeanor seemed to morph between forlorn, morose and wanton. She knew she had never been and never would be as scared as she was right at that moment. Lloyd truly was a creature, a man devoid of any basic human emotions.

In that moment Sheila recalled that the only success she'd had in dealing with Lloyd was to approach him like the sociopath he was. She decided it was her only chance to survive, so she stood up and calmly brushed the debris from her coat. She tossed her head and massaged her scalp where he had pulled her hair. *God that hurts. But stay strong, Sheila.*

She removed her coat and threw it to the side. Standing straight, she pointed at Lloyd, her hand mimicking a handgun. "Okay, Asshole. Listen close and get this. There never was going to be a you and me. And don't be calling Benno a pissant. He's twice the man you'll ever be. And one more thing. Don't wave that fricking, stupid spider tattoo at me anymore. It makes me sick." She pointed at the pistol Lloyd was holding at his side. "I think the best thing you can do with that is to put the barrel in your mouth and pull the trigger. That would do us all a huge favor. So what's it going to be, Asshole? You going to blow your brains out, or are you going to continue trying to escape? Whatever you decide, I want you to know that I'm not leaving here." She nodded in the direction the helicopter had taken. "You know there are people who will be here shortly and they're going to get you, Lloyd. There's no getting away."

Sheila refused to blink or to look away knowing that her strength and resolve would be lost. She stared deep into the abyss of her captor's evilness.

Finally, Lloyd raised the Ruger and used the front sight blade to scratch his temple. "Like I told you before, Bitch, you got yourself some set of balls. More so than that pissant, sorry excuse of a man, Benno. So the question is, what am I goin' to do with you? Cuz I sure as hell ain't leavin' you to tell anyone anything."

His snarl vanished and he turned his head and stared into the woods. "Now what the hell was that?"

CHAPTER 48

Charlie set the red and white SAR helicopter down in a clearing close to where Brendan had left the four-wheelers. Before Charlie could put the chopper into idle mode, Noslo and Troy, the two volunteers, were trotting into the campsite with their medical bags. Ira had his arms around Peter and Vickie, and Susan was holding Brendan, whose head was drooped against her chest.

"Thank God you're here. I'm Rabbi Ira Jacobson and these folks are the Brownlee family. I think you will need to direct your immediate attention to Mr. Brownlee. He was worked over pretty good by Lloyd, and he's not responding very well." Ira looked at the children. "Now you guys go to your mom and try to help her, and these folks will take care of your dad. Okay? These people are going to get you all out of here, and I'll catch up with you later."

Noslo and Troy knelt next to Brendan and began their assessments while Ira walked over to meet Charlie, who was trotting toward them. Ira extended his right hand. "I'm Rabbi Ira Jacobson, and like I told your team members, thank God you're here. The gentleman, Mr. Brownlee, is seriously injured and is going to need some urgent medical attention. Can you take his wife and their children with you?"

"Of course. But what about you?"

"Lloyd has taken my friend Sheila as a hostage, and I'm going to see if I can find them. Lloyd's partner, Benno, left here right before you landed, and he's armed as well. I can't let anything happen to Sheila."

"An FBI agent and two others will be here shortly, and they're trained for this sort of mission. Why don't you wait and allow them to pursue those felons? Or go with them at least?" He pointed to the west. "One of those guys shot at us, so you gotta know they're extremely dangerous."

"I know they are. And that's why I'm leaving now. You can tell the FBI agent that I've left and which direction I went."

Ira adjusted his yarmulke and began his pursuit of Lloyd and Sheila. She had caused him to experience emotions he had not previously encountered, and he needed to rescue her.

NUBE, ROBERTO AND JESSE entered the campsite on Wild Bill Lake as Noslo and Troy were securing the straps on the gurney holding a man who had bandages on his head and his hands. An IV bag and tubing was connected to each arm, and an oxygen cannula extended from the man's nose to a small tank attached to the side of the gurney. There were also wires from his chest to an EKG monitor tucked between his left arm and the gurney. A disheveled lady with torn clothes and a swollen face was standing off to the side holding her hands over her mouth. Two children were crying and holding onto her.

"Charlie!"

The third man was walking toward the awaiting helicopter, whose blades were stirring up a cloud of dust. He turned with a questioning look on his face before recognizing his longtime friend. "Hey, Rob. Good to see you." He nodded at his two assistants, who were pushing the gurney toward the chopper. "As you can see, I can't chat long. I will tell you that a rabbi was here, and I tried to convince him to wait for you guys. But he said some bad ass named Lloyd, not his exact words, had some lady friend of his and he was going after them. He also said that another guy—I believe his name was Benno, and I assume he is the other felon—left here just before we landed. He said this Benno dude was armed. And I know that Lloyd character is armed because he fired some big-ass handgun at us. I don't know how he missed, but thank God he did." Charlie pointed in the direction Ira had gone. "The rabbi headed in that direction."

He looked at the SAR chopper. His two assistants had the victim, the lady, and the two children inside and strapped in. Roberto accepted Charlie's outstretched hand in a quick, firm shake. "Sorry I can't chat some more, Rob, but we gotta go. Good luck and talk to you soon."

Charlie ducked under the whirling blades and entered the Sikorsky. Within thirty seconds they could see the cardinal red underside as the chopper lifted off and banked to the north.

Roberto watched until the helicopter was out of sight before looking at Nube and Jesse. "You guys hear what he said?"

Nube and Jesse nodded. "Well, let's go find them," Roberto said. "What this Lloyd doesn't know is that he's headed toward a huge gorge. It has a steep drop of about eight hundred feet and is about two hundred yards across with a fast-running stream running through the bottom. Great for trout, but hell for anyone who wants to cross it and doesn't know where to go or how to get to the bottom." Roberto looked at Nube. "Well, my friend, how do you want to do this?"

Nube repositioned his backpack and held his rifle. "Remember what we talked about, at your home, before leaving on this mission, Rob. This is an FBI pursuit and apprehension mission and not a vigilante vendetta mission. We will do our best to apprehend and return these felons to justice so they can stand trial for their crimes." Nube smiled. "Unless they fire upon us first. Agreed?"

Roberto waited long enough before responding to see if he could make the young FBI agent nervous. When he realized he couldn't, he said, "Agreed. Now let's head out."

Nube held up his hand. "One more thing, Rob. When we find them, I would suggest that you two"—he pointed at Roberto and Jesse—"take flank positions and I will continue the straightforward approach. Okay?"

When they both nodded, Nube looked at Roberto. "Okay, Chief. Lead us onward."

CHAPTER 49

Benno had been able to see Lloyd and Sheila standing in a clearing for the last twenty-five yards of his approach. However, when he stepped on a dead twig, he could tell Lloyd had heard it. He had become immediately alarmed and was staring in Benno's direction waving the .44 magnum around like it was some toy. Sheila appeared frightened, but in some surreal way she also seemed composed.

Benno trembled at the sight of his so-called friend, the man who had beaten him and left him for dead. He also became acutely aware that the pain from his injuries had begun to intensify once again. At that moment Benno wasn't sure if he was ready, or strong enough, to confront Lloyd.

He took a deep breath and was ready to approach them. "Now what the hell was that?" Lloyd yelled.

Lloyd grabbed Sheila by the arm with such force that she almost fell. "Let's go. We're leavin'! And you're comin' with me!"

Sheila attempted to wrestle from his grip. "Get your dirty hands off me! I told you that I'm not going anywhere with you and that I'm staying right here!"

Lloyd whirled around and pushed the muzzle of the .44 under her nose. "Listen, Bitch. I ain't got no time to be discussin' bullshit with you. Like I told you and that pissant Benno, I call the shots around here! Not some snot-nosed, pushy bitch! Understand?"

He pulled her with such intensity that she stumbled. She regained her balance and began striking his arm. "I said let go of me, you son of a bitch!"

Lloyd stopped so suddenly that Sheila bumped into him. The look on his face was one she had not seen. Lloyd's voice was like a growled whisper, but he seemed to emphasize each word. He squinted so that his eyebrows were almost uninterrupted, like a long, misplaced mustache. And his eyes, although empty, were the epitome of evil. The single forehead crease again created a sine wave appearance. In that brief moment, Sheila was positive she was going to die.

Lloyd pushed the muzzle of the magnum handgun under Sheila's chin with enough force to tilt her head back. "You are comin' with me. Understand? No more questions. Remember, I've got two bullets left in this little baby. Now, let's go." He pulled her again with enough force that she stumbled a few steps.

BENNO COULDN'T HEAR the entire exchange between Lloyd and Sheila, but he could see the look on Lloyd's face. He didn't need to hear him to know what he was saying. When Lloyd grabbed Sheila's arm and pulled her behind him, Benno stepped out from behind the tree and resumed his pursuit.

IRA THOUGHT HE detected movement ahead of him, and then he saw Benno step out from behind a tree. He was about to call out to him when he saw the handgun in Benno's hand. Thinking that discretion was the better part of valor, he decided to hasten his pursuit, but he attempted to do so as quietly as he could.

"SHIT! NOW WHAT THE HELL IS THIS?" Lloyd peered down from the edge of the deepest gorge he had ever seen. "How the hell are we goin' to get down there?"

He pulled Sheila to his side and loosened his grip on her arm. Sheila thought he looked like a small, lost, confused little boy. "You got any ideas how we're goin' to get down there? And don't give me none of that bullshit about not goin'"

"Well, Lloyd. You surprise me. You just told me that you make all the decisions and that I was just a dumb bitch. And now you're asking me for help?" She grabbed his arm and he released his grip. "I'll tell you what I'm going to do. I'm going to sit down right here and wait for the smart one in our group to decide what we're going to do next." She sat down, cross-legged, and began to tap the ground with a small stick. After a moment she gazed up at Lloyd, who was staring into the abyss before them. "I'm waiting, oh wise one."

Lloyd squatted and faced her. "You got your choice." He pointed the .44 between her eyes. "I can shoot you, or…" He pointed, with the handgun, at the gorge. "You can come with me. And you're goin' to go first cuz I don't want you throwin' no stones or somethin' at me on the way down. Your choice. What'll it be, Bitch?"

Sheila was contemplating her fate when she heard, "Lloyd! You hear me, you son of a bitch?"

Sheila jerked her head toward the voice but Lloyd, recognizing Benno's voice, calmly turned. He stood up and the smile faded away. "Well, well, little man. So you didn't die after all. Guess I gotta give you more credit than I thought you deserved." He looked around for Benno while waving the Ruger. "So, you gonna hide or are you gonna come out and join our party? Me and the bitch here are just tryin' to figure out how to get to the bottom of this big-ass hole."

Benno stepped out from behind a tree and walked toward Lloyd and Sheila. He pointed the .38 at Lloyd. "It's over, Lloyd. Let the lady go. It's just you and me. Just like always, huh, Partner?" He said the last word with a sneer.

"You think you got the balls to fire that? You think you can shoot me, you little pissant?"

Benno continued walking toward his former cell-mate. "I got two bullets in here, Lloyd, and one has your name on it." He stopped when he was ten feet from Lloyd.

"Benno! Lloyd! Hold on a minute!"

The two felons and Sheila turned at the sound of Ira's voice. Ira walked into the small clearing holding his hands up. "There's no need for any more violence. You've got what you want." He nodded toward the moneybag that Lloyd had set down by his side. "Why don't you let Sheila go? She and I will attempt to find our own way out of here, and you two can continue your escape to wherever it is you want to go."

With his arms still raised he asked, "What do you say? Does that sound all right to you two?" He dropped his left hand and reached toward Sheila without losing eye contact with Lloyd.

"Let's let 'em go, Lloyd. It can still be just me and you. Like always. We don't need to hurt 'em. Besides, what the hell can they tell anybody that they don't already know? Know what I mean, huh?"

"Benno, Benno, Benno. I knew it and said it before. You got somethin' for the lady, don't ya?"

"No I don't, Lloyd."

Lloyd pulled the hammer back on the Ruger and pointed it at Benno. "Like I've always told ya, you talk too much. I only got two bullets left, and this is what I'm gonna do. I'm goin' to push these two sorry assholes, the preacher man and the bitch, over the side of this cliff. Then I'm goin' to shoot you, and I'll have one left, plus whatever you got in that pea shooter, to defend myself when some other assholes try to take me in."

Lloyd swung the handgun toward Ira and Sheila. "Now you two start. . ."

The sound of the .38 exploding, although diminutive in comparison to the .44, sounded like a cannon echoing across the expanse of the gorge. Lloyd's left arm fell useless to his side, and a blood pattern began to form over his shoulder.

Sheila screamed and Ira dropped to her side, placing himself between her and their captors.

Lloyd dropped to one knee and turned toward Benno. "Son of a bitch, that hurts. But I gotta give it to you, little man. You do got some balls after all. But now I'm gonna return you the favor."

Lloyd fired the magnum, striking Benno in the left shoulder. The force of the 240-grain bullet spun Benno around and threw him to the ground. He lost his grip on the .38 Ruger, and it landed at the feet of Ira, who stared at it for a moment before picking it up. He had never held a gun of any type in his life and wasn't sure how to fire it.

Ira held the pistol in both hands and stood up, keeping himself between Sheila and Lloyd, who was still on one knee. Lloyd's pained expression was replaced by a snarl. He stood up and raised his handgun. "Now what you goin' to do with that, Preacher Man?"

"Malin! This is Agent Lawson with the FBI! Drop your weapon, get on your knees, and place your hands on your head! It's over, Malin! You're surrounded, so give it up!"

Nube walked into the clearing holding his Glock 22 .40-caliber handgun extended in front of him with both hands. He continued to approach the fugitive. "I have agents on either side of you, Malin, so drop your weapon, get on your knees and place your hands on your head. Now!"

Lloyd's snarl returned and he began to raise his handgun. "Go f—"

For the second time within minutes, the .38 exploded and Lloyd Malin dropped like a poleaxed steer. Ira stood holding the still-smoking pistol in trembling hands. He stared at it for a moment and threw it on the ground. He dropped to both knees and held his head in his hands. He looked up and put his hands together. "My God, what have I done?"

Sheila wrapped her arms around his neck. "You saved our lives, Ira. That's what you've done." She kissed him on the cheek and laid her head on his shoulder. "Thank you, Ira."

Roberto and Jesse emerged from the woods with their handguns extended and converged on the downed fugitives. Nube was kneeling next to Lloyd and had thrown the .44 to the side. He looked at Roberto. "This one's alive. Hurt, but alive. How about you check on the other one?" He turned toward Jesse. "And how about you take care of the rabbi and the lady." He grinned. "And take that gun away from him."

It only took a few minutes to assess the wounds, apply some bandages, and secure Malin and Donnrud with handcuffs. Nube had some morphine ampoules in his first aid kit, but decided not to administer it. These two felons had to walk back to the clearing to be extricated. Besides, perhaps in some perverse moment, he didn't think their wounds were that bad.

"How are the rabbi and the lady, Jess?"

"The lady is fine. She is one cool lady. The rabbi is a little shook up after not only firing a weapon for the first time in his life, but shooting someone. But he'll be okay."

"Rob, if you'll keep an eye on these two…" He pointed at Lloyd and Benno. "I'll call Agent Benson and apprise him of our status and ask him to have Charlie return with the chopper and pick us up at that campsite where he landed before. As soon as I'm finished, we'll head out. And, by the way, thanks for your help."

Roberto put his arm around Jesse and kissed the top of her head. "It was our pleasure, Agent Lawson."

CHAPTER 50

It had been two weeks since the Malin-Donnrud mission had been completed. Clyde had recovered sufficiently to be discharged from the hospital so the group, including Bogey and Britches and Nube's shorthair, Ms. Abby, were gathered at Roberto's for a celebratory dinner. Roberto held up his glass of Merlot and nodded toward his dear friend. "Here's to you, Clyde."

"Here, here!" Nube and Jesse said in unison.

"Shucks, why are you guys toasting me? You did all the work." Clyde looked at Nube. "By the way, you never did finish telling me the story of those two. What happened to 'em? They get the book thrown at 'em, I hope?"

Nube grinned at Roberto, knowing they had already told Clyde the story, but he thought the old gentleman probably loved to hear stories again and again.

Nube took a long drink of his Cabernet, set the glass down, and stared at it while he twirled the stem in his fingers. He stared at the dark red liquid as it raced toward the lip of the glass only to slide back down. For a moment he thought this represented the FBI, an attempted escape, but captured. He knew he was stalling while trying to put on a serious FBI face before looking up. "Well, Clyde, it was like this. . ."

Nube began reciting the saga of Lloyd and Benno again. Occasionally he would halt his narrative and take a drink from his glass of wine which seemed, mysteriously, to always be full. And then he would stare off as if he wanted to ensure that his recounting of the apprehension was exact. Nube thought he could sense Clyde sliding forward on his chair each time he halted, and at one point he began to wonder if he would fall off.

He told Clyde that after securing the fugitives and talking to his boss, Agent Benson had dispatched Charlie Brayer and his SAR chopper to the Wild Bill Lake campsite. The felons were examined and treated in the Good Shepherd Hospital emergency room. The ER doc said their wounds were not considered serious enough to warrant hospitalization, so they were remanded over to the custody of the Billings Police Department. They were offered public defenders and were scheduled for arraignment.

The DA said they would be charged, under Montana law, with felony murder as well as armed robbery and kidnapping, but they would also face federal charges on kidnapping. Nube went on to tell Clyde he thought Lloyd would go away for life and that maybe, and it was a big maybe, Benno may receive a lighter sentence because he attempted to assist Ira and Sheila and prevented them from being murdered.

Clyde took a small sip of his Riesling before repositioning himself on his chair. "I love that story, Nube. And, I admit, you have told me the story before. So thank you for humoring an old man." Clyde directed his attention to Roberto. "Now you tell me, Rob, how you got my four-wheeler back. And what happened to my Ruger .44 magnum? That was a gift from my wife, you know."

"Clyde, I've told you before about your four-wheeler. And I also told you the FBI has given me your pistol and as soon as I get it cleaned up, I'll give it back." Roberto looked at Jesse. "May I ask how our dinner is coming, or are we just going to drink all night?"

Jesse stood and saluted Roberto. "Yes, Sir. I'll get right on it, Sir." She took a step toward the kitchen to check on the pot roast in the oven. "None of you has asked about

Ira and Sheila. So let me give you an update. I spoke with Sheila today, and guess what?" The three men stared at her without responding. "Well, they are starting to see each other socially. She said they've got that whole religion thing to work through, but she is excited. I think she really likes him. And for you relationship deficient minded men, I do believe he likes her as well." She lifted her glass. "So here's to at least one potential couple."

Nube looked at Roberto. "What was that last part all about?"

"I think part of it was directed at me." He pointed at Nube. "And I think part of it was directed at you."

From the kitchen they heard, "Very perceptive, DeLaCroix." Jesse came back to the table. "Remember at our first camp along the river, Nube, when you were telling us about Nancy?"

He smiled. He thought he knew where this was headed. "Yes. I remember telling you about her."

Jesse took another healthy swallow of wine. "Well, just what in the hell are you going to do about it, Mr. Fed Man?"

"How's your wine doing there, Deputy?" Roberto asked.

Jesse glared down at him. "Never you mind, you relationshipless man. So, Nube. What are you going to do?"

Nube leaned back in his chair. "What would you suggest I do, Jess?"

She pointed at the phone. "I would suggest, and strongly encourage, you to get off your duff and call that woman before someone with a half-ounce of brains beats you to the punch. That is, if they haven't already. Dinner will be a few minutes yet, so you go call her." She pointed at the phone again. "Now, Nube."

Roberto put his hand on her arm. "Take it easy, Jess. I'm sure Nube will call her in his own time."

She glared at him and a tear began to form at the corner of her eye. "Like you know all about these things, Rob." She grabbed the bottle of Merlot and filled her glass, spilling some on the tablecloth. She turned toward the kitchen, and Nube could see her dabbing at the tear that was finding its way through her mascara and down her cheek.

Nube took a sip of his wine and pushed his chair back. "If you don't mind, I think I'll step outside a moment and make a phone call."

As Nube was leaving the table, Roberto glanced at Clyde, who smiled and nodded toward the kitchen. Roberto pointed at himself and mouthed, "Me?"

"Yes you, Son."

Roberto shrugged, took a deep breath, and pushed the chair away from the table. He walked up behind Jesse, who was standing at the sink staring out the window. He put his arms around her and kissed the top of her head. "How you doing, Jess?"

She shrugged and dabbed at another escaping tear.

Roberto gazed out the window and began to realize how much he cared for this lady. He turned her around and used a tissue to wipe the tears and streaking mascara from her face. He lifted her chin and lightly kissed her on the lips. "Hey. Remember that night, at our first campsite, when we began our pursuit? You know, the one you mentioned to Nube? Remember?"

"Yeah, I remember. So what about it?"

"It seems to me that we talked, I mean you mentioned, all of us going on a road trip. Remember?"

She grabbed another tissue, dabbed a tear, and blew her nose. "So?"

"So how about when Nube comes back in, we start making plans?"

Jesse stared at him as if to ask where that came from. Roberto tilted her chin a bit higher. "I care for you, Jesse. A lot. And I would really like to give you and me a good shot." He took a step back and wiped his brow. "Jesse, I'm really out of practice at this sort of thing, and. . ."

She reached up and put her finger on his lips and began to smile. "That's all you had to say, you big oaf. Now how about you get out of my kitchen so I can finish getting dinner ready." He turned to walk back toward the table and a beaming Clyde. "And one more thing, Rob." Roberto glanced over his shoulder. Jesse was holding up her empty wine glass. "I'd like another glass of wine, please."

Roberto had filled her glass and his and stood in the kitchen while Jesse carved the pot roast. Nube walked in and his smile lit up the room like a halogen light on a moonless night. He stood at the table with his hands on his chair and smiled.

"Well, Son," Clyde said. "Are you going to tell us, or are you just going to stand there with that silly grin on your face?"

"Nancy is just fine, and she says to say hi to everyone. And PJ is doing well also. He was really excited to talk to me. His golf game is improving and..." Nube did a fist pump. "Nancy wants to see me again! Soon!"

Clyde patted Nube's hand and Roberto and Jesse gave him a hug. Roberto brought the platter of food to the table, and the four waited while Clyde said grace. Nube reached for the platter.

"I want to propose another toast," Roberto said. They raised their glasses and he looked at Clyde. "To a dear friend." Then he turned to Nube. "To a new friend." He turned to Jesse, who had tears streaming down her face. He put his free hand on hers and tipped his glass toward her. "And to my soon-to-be best friend."

She smiled through her tears of joy and mouthed, "Thank you."

Nube looked at the group. "Now pass the platter and let's talk about a road trip."